"I'm Sorry To Disappoint, But You're Stuck With Me Today."

Gavin had screwed up last night, he could tell. Not in seducing her—that would never be a bad idea—but in forcing the idea of the apartment on her. Anyone else would jump at the offer, but to her, it was him imposing on her. Demanding they be closer so he could see his son more easily. Not once mentioning that he'd like *her* closer as well because that opened the door to dangerous territory.

Sabine was skittish. She scared off easily last time. He wasn't about to tell her that he wanted to see her more, because he was still fighting himself over the idea of it. He was usually pretty good at keeping his distance from people, but he'd already let Sabine in once. Keeping her out the second time was harder than he expected.

"That's scarcely a hardship," he said. "I find your company to be incredibly...*stimulating*."

* * *

His Lover's Little Secret is part of the #1 bestselling miniseries from Harlequin Desire—

Billionaires & Babies: Powerful men...wrapped around their babies' little fingers.

* * *

If you're on Twitter,
tell us what you think of Harlequin Desire!
#harlequindesire

Dear Reader,

Back when I was writing *More Than He Expected,* one of the secondary characters popped out to me. Sabine was quirky with purple hair, a yoga mat and a nose piercing. Not your typical Harlequin Desire heroine. But I felt like she had a story, and bits of her past came out over the course of the book—her young son; the rich, powerful father who didn't know about him... I knew I had to write her book, as well.

Figuring out who Gavin was proved to be both a joy and a challenge. He's got a hard candy coating with a soft center. Sabine helps him break out of his shell and be more than just what is expected of him.

I'm pleased to finally share Sabine and Gavin's story. If you enjoy it, tell me by visiting my website at www.andrealaurence.com, like my fan page on Facebook or follow me on Twitter.

Enjoy,

Andrea

HIS LOVER'S LITTLE SECRET

—

ANDREA LAURENCE

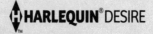

Recycling programs
for this product may
not exist in your area.

ISBN-13: 978-0-373-73308-8

HIS LOVER'S LITTLE SECRET

Copyright © 2014 by Andrea Laurence

Printed in U.S.A.

Books by Andrea Laurence

Harlequin Desire

Other titles by this author available in ebook format.

ANDREA LAURENCE

is an award-winning contemporary romance author who has been a lover of books and writing stories since she learned to read. She always dreamed of seeing her work in print and is thrilled to be able to share her books with the world. A dedicated West Coast girl transplanted into the Deep South, she's working on her own "happily ever after" with her boyfriend and five fur-babies. You can contact Andrea at her website: www.andrealaurence.com.

This book is dedicated to single mothers everywhere, including my own hard-working mother, Meg. You fight the good fight every day, often at the expense of your own well-being. Thank you for everything you do. (Treat yourself to some chocolate or shoes every now and then!)

One

"You'd better get on out of here, or you'll be late to stand on your head."

Sabine Hayes looked up from the cash drawer to see her boss, fashion designer Adrienne Lockhart Taylor, standing at the counter. She had worked for Adrienne the past thirteen months as manager of her boutique. "I'm almost done."

"Give me the nightly deposit and go. I'll stay until Jill shows up for her shift and then I'll stop by the bank on my way home. You have to pick up Jared by six, don't you?"

"Yes." The day care center would price gouge her for every minute she was late. Then she had to get Jared home and fed before the babysitter got there. Sabine loved teaching yoga, but it made those evenings even more hectic than usual. Single motherhood wasn't for wimps. "You don't mind making the deposit?"

Adrienne leaned across the counter. "Go," she said.

Sabine glanced quickly at her watch. "Okay." She put the deposit into the bank pouch and handed it over. Thank goodness Adrienne had come by this afternoon to put together the new window display. The trendy boutique was known for its exciting and edgy displays that perfectly showcased Adrienne's flair for modern pinup girl fashions. Sabine couldn't have found a better place to work.

Most places wouldn't look twice at an applicant with a nose piercing and a stripe of blue in her hair. It didn't matter that it was a small, tasteful diamond stud or that her hair was dyed at a nice salon in Brooklyn. Even after she'd bitten the bullet and had the bright color removed and left the piercing at home, she'd been turned down by every store on Fifth Avenue. The businesses that paid enough for her to support her son in New York were flooded with applicants more experienced than she was.

She thanked her lucky stars for the day she spied Adrienne walking down the street and complimented her dress. She never expected her to say she'd designed it herself. Adrienne invited her to come by her new boutique one afternoon, and Sabine was enamored with the whole place. It was fun and funky, chic and stylish. High-class fashion with an edge. When Adrienne mentioned she was looking for someone to run the store so she could focus on her designs, Sabine couldn't apply fast enough. Not only was it a great job with above-average pay and benefits, Adrienne was a great boss. She didn't care what color hair Sabine had—now she had purple highlights—and she was understanding when child illness or drama kept her away from the store.

Sabine grabbed her purse and gave a quick wave to

Adrienne as she disappeared into the stockroom and out the back door. It was only a couple blocks to her son's day care, but she still had to hurry along the sidewalk, brushing past others who were leisurely making their way around town.

Finally rounding the last corner, Sabine swung open the gate to the small courtyard and leaped up the few steps to the door. She rang the buzzer at exactly three minutes to six. Not long after that, she had her toddler in her arms and was on her way to the subway.

"Hey, buddy," she said as they went down the street. "Did you have a good day?"

Jared grinned and nodded enthusiastically. He was starting to lose his chubby baby cheeks. He'd grown so much the past few months. Every day, he looked more and more like his father. The first time she'd held Jared in her arms, she looked into his dark brown eyes and saw Gavin's face staring back at her. He would grow up to be as devastatingly handsome as his father, but hopefully with Sabine's big heart. She should be able to contribute *something* to the genetic makeup of her child, and if she had her pick, that was what it would be.

"What do you want for dinner tonight?"

"A-sketti."

"Spaghetti, again? You had that last night. You're going to turn into a noodle before too long."

Jared giggled and clung to her neck. Sabine breathed in the scent of his baby shampoo and pressed a kiss against his forehead. He had changed her whole life and she wouldn't trade him for anything.

"Sabine?"

The subway entrance was nearly in sight when someone called her name from the restaurant she'd just passed. She stopped and turned to find a man in a navy suit drinking wine at one of the tables on the sidewalk. He looked familiar, but she couldn't come up with his name. Where did she know him from?

"It is you," he said, standing up and stepping toward her. He took one look at her puzzled expression and smiled. "You don't remember me, do you? I'm Clay Oliver, a friend of Gavin's. I met you at a gallery opening a couple years back."

An icy surge rushed through Sabine's veins. She smiled and nodded, trying not to show any outward signs of distress. "Oh, yes," she said. She shifted Jared in her arms so he was facing away from his father's best friend. "I think I spilled champagne on you, right?"

"Yes!" he said, pleased she remembered. "How have you been?" Clay's gaze ran curiously over the child in her arms. "Busy, I see."

"Yes, very busy." Sabine's heart began pounding loudly in her chest. She glanced over her shoulder at the subway stop, desperate for an escape. "Listen, I'm sorry I can't stay to chat longer, but I've got to meet the babysitter. It was good to see you again, Clay. Take care."

Sabine gave him a quick wave and spun on her heel. She felt as if she was fleeing the scene of a crime as she dashed down the stairs. She nervously watched the people joining her on the platform. Clay wouldn't follow her. At least she didn't think so. But she wouldn't feel better until she was deep into Brooklyn and far out of Gavin's sphere of influence.

Had Clay seen Jared closely enough? Had he noticed the resemblance? Jared was wearing his favorite monkey T-shirt with a hood and ears, so perhaps Clay hadn't been able to make out his features or how old he was. She hoped.

She leaped onto the train the moment it arrived and managed to find a seat. Clutching Jared tightly as he sat in her lap, she tried to breathe deeply, but she just couldn't do it.

Nearly three years. Jared was fewer than two months from his second birthday, and she had managed to keep their son a secret from Gavin. In all this time she'd never run into him or anyone he knew. They didn't exactly move in the same social circles. That was part of why she'd broken it off with Gavin. They were a world apart. Unsuitable in every way. After she split with him, he'd never called or texted her again. He obviously wasn't missing her too badly.

But Sabine had never allowed herself to relax. She knew that sooner or later, Gavin would find out that he had a son. If Clay didn't tell him tonight, it would be the next time she bumped into someone Gavin knew. Sitting in the park, walking down the street…somebody would see Jared and know instantly that he was Gavin's son. The bigger he got, the more of a carbon copy of his father he became.

Then it was only a matter of time before Gavin showed up, angry and demanding. That was how he worked. He always got his way. At least until now. The only thing Sabine knew for certain was that he wouldn't win this time. Jared was her son. *Hers.* Gavin was a workaholic and wouldn't have a clue what to do with a child. She wasn't about to turn him over to the stuffy nannies and boarding schools that had raised Gavin instead of his parents.

As the train approached their stop, Sabine got up and

they hurried to catch the bus that would take them the last few blocks to her apartment near Marine Park in Brooklyn, where she'd lived the past four years. It wasn't the fanciest place in the world, but it was relatively safe, clean and close to the grocery store and the park. The one-bedroom apartment was growing smaller as Jared grew older, but they were managing.

Originally, a large portion of the bedroom was used as her art studio. When her son came along, she packed up her canvases and put her artistic skills toward painting a cheerful mural over his crib. Jared had plenty of room to play, and there was a park down the street where he could run around and dig in the sandbox. Her next-door neighbor, Tina, would watch Jared when she had her evening yoga classes.

She had put together a pretty good life for her and Jared. Considering that when she moved to New York she was broke and homeless, she'd come quite a long way. Back then, she could live on meager waitressing tips and work on her paintings when she had the extra money for supplies. Now, she had to squeeze out every penny she could manage, but they had gotten by.

"A-sketti!" Jared cheered triumphantly as they came through the door.

"Okay. I'll make a-sketti." Sabine sat him down before switching the television on to his favorite show. It would mesmerize him with songs and funny dances while she cooked.

By the time Jared was done eating and Sabine was changed into her workout clothes, she had only minutes to spare before Tina arrived. If she was lucky, Tina would give Jared a bath and scrub the tomato sauce off his cheeks. Usually, she had him in his pajamas and in bed by the time Sabine got home. Sabine hated that he would be asleep when she returned, but going through his nightly routine after class would have Jared up way past his bedtime. He'd wake up at dawn no matter what, but he'd be cranky.

There was a sharp knock at the door. Tina was a little early. That was fine by her. If she could catch the earlier bus, it would give her enough time to get some good stretches in before class.

"Hey, Tina—" she said, whipping open the door and momentarily freezing when her petite, middle-aged neighbor was not standing in the hallway.

No. No, no, no. She wasn't ready to deal with this. Not yet. Not tonight.

It was Gavin.

Sabine clutched desperately at the door frame, needing its support to keep her upright as the world started tilting sharply on its axis. Her chest tightened; her stomach churned and threatened to return her dinner. At the same time, other long-ignored parts of her body immediately sparked back to life. Gavin had always been a master of her body, and the years hadn't dulled the memory of his touch.

Fear. Desire. Panic. Need. It all swirled inside her like a building maelstrom that would leave nothing but destruction in its path. She took a deep breath to clamp it all down. She couldn't let Gavin know she was freaking out. She certainly couldn't let him know she still responded to him, either. That would give him the upper hand. She plastered a wide smile across her face and choked down her emotions.

"Hello, Sabine," he said with the deep, familiar voice she remembered.

It was hard to believe the handsome and rich blast from her past was standing in front of her after all this time. His flawlessly tailored gray suit and shiny, sky-blue tie made him look every inch the powerful CEO of the BXS shipping empire. His dark eyes were trained on her, his gaze traveling down the line of his nose. He looked a little older than she remembered, with concern lining his eyes and furrowing his brow. Or maybe it was the tense, angry expression that aged him.

"Gavin!" she said with feigned surprise. "I certainly didn't expect to see you here. I thought you were my neighbor Tina. How have you—"

"Where is my son?" he demanded, interrupting her nervous twitter. His square jaw was rock hard, his sensual lips pressed into a hard line of disapproval. There had been a flash of that same expression when she'd left him all those years ago, but he'd quickly grown indifferent to it. Now he cared. But not about her. Only about their child.

Apparently news traveled fast. It had been fewer than two hours since she'd run into Clay.

"Your son?" she repeated, hoping to stall long enough to think of a plan. She'd had years to prepare for this moment and yet, when it arrived, she was thrown completely off guard. Moving quickly, Sabine rushed into the hallway and pulled the apartment door nearly closed behind her. She left just the slightest crack open so she could peek through and make sure Jared was okay. She pressed her back against the door frame and found it calmed her nerves just a little to have that barrier between Gavin and Jared. He'd have to go through her to get inside.

"Yes, Sabine," Gavin said, taking a step closer to her. "Where is the baby you've hidden from me for the last three years?"

* * *

Damn, she was still as beautiful as he remembered. A little older, a little curvier, but still the fresh, funky artist that had turned his head in that art gallery. And tonight, she was wearing some skimpy workout clothes that clung to every newly rounded curve and reminded him of what he'd been missing since she'd walked out on him.

People tended not to stay in Gavin's life very long. There had been a parade of nannies, tutors, friends and lovers his whole life as his parents hired and fired and then moved him from one private school to the next. The dark-haired beauty with the nose piercing had been no exception. She had walked out of his life without a second thought.

She'd said they weren't compatible in the long term because they had different priorities and different lives. Admittedly, they fell on opposite ends of the spectrum in most every category, but that was one of the things he'd been drawn to in Sabine. One of the reasons he thought she, of all people, might stay. She wasn't just another rich girl looking to marry well and shop often. What they had really seemed to matter. To mean something.

He'd been wrong.

He'd let her go—he'd learned early that there was no sense in chasing after someone who didn't want to be there—but she'd stayed on his mind. She'd starred in his dreams, both erotic and otherwise. She'd crept into his thoughts during the quiet moments when he had time to regret the past. More than once, Gavin had wondered what Sabine was up to and what she had done with her life.

Never in his wildest dreams did he expect the answer to be "raising his child."

Sabine straightened her spine, her sharp chin tipping up in defiance. She projected an air of confidence in any situation and had the steel backbone to stand behind it. She certainly had spunk; he'd loved that about her once. Now, he could tell it would be an annoyance.

She looked him straight in the eye and said, "He's inside. And right now, that's where he's staying."

The bold honesty of her words was like a fist to his gut. The air rushed from his lungs. It was true. He had a son. *A son!* He hadn't entirely believed Clay's story until that precise moment. He'd known his best friend since they were roommates in college, one of the few constants in his life, but he couldn't always trust Clay's version of reality. Tonight, he'd insisted that Gavin locate Sabine as soon as possible to find out about her young son.

And he'd been right. For once.

Sabine didn't deny it. He'd expected her to tell him it wasn't his child or insist she was babysitting for a friend, but she had always been honest to a fault. Instead, she'd flat-out admitted she'd hidden his child from him and made no apologies about it. She even had the audacity to start making demands about how this was going to go down. She'd been in control of this situation for far too long. He was about to be included and in a big way.

"He's really my son?" He needed to hear the words from her, although he would demand a DNA test to confirm it no matter what she said.

Sabine swallowed and nodded. "He looks just like you."

The blood started pumping furiously in Gavin's ears. He might be able to understand why she kept it a secret if she was uncertain he was the father, but there was no doubt in her mind. She simply hadn't wanted him involved. She didn't want the inconvenience of having to share him with someone else. If not for Clay seeing her, he still wouldn't know he had a child.

His jaw tightened and his teeth clenched together. "Were you ever going to tell me I had a son, Sabine?"

Her pale green gaze burrowed into him as she crossed her arms over her chest. "No."

She didn't even bother to lie about it and make herself look less like the deceitful, selfish person she was. She just stood there, looking unapologetic, while unconsciously pressing her breasts up out of the top of her sports bra. His brain flashed between thoughts like a broken television as his eyes ran over the soft curves of her body and his ears tried to process her response. Anger, desire, betrayal and a fierce need to possess her rushed through his veins, exploding out of him in words.

"What do you mean, no?" Gavin roared.

"Keep it down!" Sabine demanded between gritted teeth, glancing nervously over her shoulder into the apartment. "I don't want him to hear us, and I certainly don't want all my neighbors to hear us, either."

"Well I'm sorry to embarrass you in front of your neighbors. I just found out I have a two-year-old son that I've never met. I think that gives me the right to be angry."

Sabine took a deep breath, amazing him with her ability to appear so calm. "You have every right to be angry. But yelling won't change anything. And I won't have you raising your voice around my son."

"*Our* son," Gavin corrected.

"No," she said with a sharp point of her finger. "He's my son. According to his birth certificate, he's an immaculate conception. Right now, you have no legal claim to him and no right to tell me how to do *anything* where he's concerned. You got that?"

That situation would be remedied and soon. "For now. But don't think your selfish monopoly on our son will last for much longer."

A crimson flush rushed to her cheeks, bringing color to her flawless, porcelain skin. She had gotten far too comfortable calling the shots. He could tell she didn't like him making demands. Too bad for her. He had a vote now and it was long overdue.

She swallowed and brushed her purple-highlighted ponytail over her shoulder but didn't back down. "It's after seven-thirty on a Wednesday night, so you can safely bet that's how it's going to stay for the immediate future."

Gavin laughed at her bold naïveté. "Do you honestly think my lawyers don't answer the phone at 2:00 a.m. when I call? For what I pay them, they do what I want, when I want." He slipped his hand into his suit coat and pulled his phone out of his inner breast pocket. "Shall we call Edmund and see if he's available?"

Her eyes widened slightly at his challenge. "Go ahead, Gavin. Any lawyer worth his salt is going to insist on a DNA test. It takes no less than three days to get the results of a paternity test back from a lab. If you push me, I'll see to it that you don't set eyes on him until the results come back. If we test first thing in the morning, that would mean Monday by my estimation."

Gavin's hands curled into tight fists at his sides. She'd had years to prepare for this moment and she'd done her homework. He knew she was right. The labs probably wouldn't process the results over the weekend, so it would be Monday at the earliest before he could get his lawyer involved and start making parental demands. But once he could lay claim to his son, she had better watch out.

"I want to see my son," he said. This time his tone was less heated and demanding.

"Then calm down and take your thumb off your lawyer's speed dial."

Gavin slipped his cell phone back into his pocket. "Happy?"

Sabine didn't seem happy, but she nodded anyway. "Now, before I let you in, we need to discuss some ground rules."

He took a deep breath to choke back his rude retort. Few people had the audacity to tell him what to do, but if anyone would, it was Sabine. He would stick to her requirements for now, but before long, Gavin would be making the rules. "Yes?"

"Number one, you are not to yell when you are in my apartment or anywhere Jared might be. I don't want you upsetting him."

Jared. His son's name was Jared. This outrageous scenario was getting more and more real. "What's his middle name?" Gavin couldn't stop himself from asking. He suddenly wanted to know everything he could about his son. There was no way to gain back the time he'd lost, but he would do everything in his power to catch up on what he missed.

"Thomas. Jared Thomas Hayes."

Thomas was *his* middle name. Was that a coincidence? He couldn't remember if Sabine knew it or not. "Why Thomas?"

"For my art teacher in high school, Mr. Thomas. He's the only one that ever encouraged my painting. Since that was also your middle name, it seemed fitting. Number two," she continued. "Do not tell him you're his father. Not until it is legally confirmed and we are both comfortable with the timing. I don't want him confused and worried about what's going on."

"Who does he think his father is?"

Sabine shook her head dismissively. "He's not even two. He hasn't started asking questions about things like that yet."

"Fine," he agreed, relieved that if nothing else, his son hadn't noticed the absence of a father in his life. He knew how painful that could be. "Enough rules. I want to see Jared." His son's name felt alien on his tongue. He wanted a face to put with the name and know his son at last.

"Okay." Sabine shifted her weight against the door, slowly slinking into the apartment.

Gavin moved forward, stepping over the threshold. He'd been to her apartment before, a long time ago. He remembered a fairly sparse but eclectic space with mismatched thrift store furniture. Her paintings had dotted the walls, her portfolio and bag of supplies usually sitting near the door.

When he barely missed stepping on a chubby blue crayon instead of a paintbrush, he knew things were truly different. Looking around, he noticed a lot had changed. The furniture was newer but still a mishmash of pieces. Interspersed with it were brightly colored plastic toys like a tiny basketball hoop and a tricycle with superheroes on it. A television in the corner loudly played a children's show.

And when Sabine stepped aside, he saw the small, dark-haired boy sitting on the floor in front of it. The child didn't turn to look at him. He was immersed in bobbing his head and singing along to the song playing on the show, a toy truck clutched in his hand.

Gavin swallowed hard and took another step into the apartment so Sabine could close the door behind him. He watched her walk over to the child and crouch down.

"Jared, we have a visitor. Let's say hello."

The little boy set down his truck and crawled to his feet. When he turned to look at Gavin, he felt his heart skip a beat in his chest. The tiny boy looked exactly like he had as a child. It was as though a picture had been snatched from his baby album and brought to life. From his pink cheeks smeared with tomato sauce, to the wide, dark eyes that looked at him with curiosity, he was very much Gavin's son.

The little boy smiled, revealing tiny baby teeth. "Hi."

Gavin struggled to respond at first. His chest was tight with emotions he never expected in this moment. This morning, he woke up worried about his latest business acquisition and now he was meeting his child for the first time. "Hi, Jared," he choked out.

"Jared, this is Mommy's friend Gavin."

Gavin took a hesitant step forward and knelt down to bring himself to the child's level. "How are you doing, big guy?"

Jared responded with a flow of gibberish he couldn't understand. Gavin hadn't been around many small children, and he wasn't equipped to translate. He could pick out a few words—*school, train* and something close to *spaghetti.* The rest was lost on him, but Jared didn't seem to mind. Pausing in his tale, he picked up his favorite truck and held it out to Gavin. "My truck!" he declared.

He took the small toy from his son. "It's very nice. Thank you."

A soft knock sounded at the front door. Sabine frowned and stood up. "That's the babysitter. I've got to go."

Gavin swallowed his irritation. He'd had a whole two minutes with his son and she was trying to push him out the door. They hadn't even gotten around to discussing her actions and what they were going to do about this situation. He watched her walk to the door and let in a middle-aged woman in a sweater with cats on it.

"Hey, Tina. Come on in. He's had his dinner and he's just watching television."

"I'll get him in the bath and in bed by eight-thirty."

"Thanks, Tina. I should be home around the usual time."

Gavin handed the truck back to Jared and reluctantly stood. He wasn't going to hang around while the neighbor lady was here. He turned in time to see Sabine slip into a hoodie and tug a sling with a rolled-up exercise mat over her shoulder.

"Gavin, I've got to go. I'm teaching a class tonight."

He nodded and gave a quick look back at Jared. He'd returned to watching his show, doing a little monkey dance along with the other children and totally unaware of what was really going on around him. Gavin wanted to reach out to him again, to say goodbye or hug him, but he refrained. There would be time for all that later. For the first time in his life, he had someone who would be legally bound to him for the next sixteen years and wouldn't breeze in and out of his life like so many others. They would have more time together.

Right now, he needed to deal with the mother of his child.

Two

"I don't need you to drive me to class."

Gavin stood holding open the passenger door of his Aston Martin with a frown lining his face. Sabine knew she didn't want to get in the car with him. Getting in would mean a private tongue-lashing she wasn't ready for yet. She'd happily take the bus to avoid this.

"Just get in the car, Sabine. The longer we argue, the later you'll be."

Sabine watched the bus blow by the stop up the street and swore under her breath. She'd never make it to class in time unless she gave in and let him drive her there. Sighing in defeat, she climbed inside. Gavin closed the door and got in on his side. "Go up the block and turn right at the light," she instructed. If she could focus on directions, perhaps they'd have less time to talk about what she'd done.

She already had a miserably guilty conscience. It wasn't like she could look at Jared without thinking of Gavin. Lying to him was never something she intended to do, but the moment she found out she was pregnant, she was overcome with a fierce territorial and protective urge. She and Gavin were from different planets. He never really cared for her the way she did for him. The same would hold true for their son. Jared would be *acquired* just like any other asset of the Brooks Empire. He deserved better than that. Better than what Gavin had been given.

She did what she thought she had to do to protect her child, and she wouldn't apologize for it. "At the second light, turn left."

Gavin remained silent as they drove, unnerving her more with every minute that ticked by. She was keenly aware of the way his hands tightly gripped the leather steering wheel. The tension was evident in every muscle of his body, straining the threads of his designer suit. His smooth, square jaw was flexed as though it took everything he had to keep his emotions in check and his eyes on the road.

It was a practiced skill of Gavin's. When they were together, he always kept his feelings tamped down. The night she told him they were over, there had barely been a flicker of emotion in his eyes. Not anger. Not sadness. Not even a "don't let the door hit you on the way out." Just a solemnly resigned nod and she was dismissed from his life. He obviously never really cared for Sabine. But this might be the situation that caused him to finally blow.

When his car pulled to a stop outside the community center where she taught, he shifted into Neutral, pulled the parking brake and killed the engine. He glanced down at his Rolex. "You're early."

She was. She didn't have to be inside for another fifteen minutes. He'd driven a great deal faster than the bus and hadn't stopped every block to pick up people. It was pointless to get out of the car and stand in front of the building to wait for the previous class to end. That meant time in the car alone with Gavin. Just perfect.

After an extended silence, he spoke. "So, was I horrible to you? Did I treat you badly?" His low voice was quiet, his eyes focused not on her but on something through the windshield ahead of them.

Sabine silently groaned. Somehow she preferred the yelling to this. "Of course not."

He turned to look at her then, pinning her with his dark eyes. "Did I say or do anything while we were together to make you think I would be a bad father?"

A bad father? No. Perhaps a distracted one. A distant one. An absent one. Or worse, a reluctant one. But not a *bad* father. "No. Gavin, I—"

"Then why, Sabine? Why would you keep something so important from me? Why would you keep me from being in Jared's life? He's young now, but eventually he'd notice he didn't have a daddy like other kids. What if he thought I didn't want him? Christ, Sabine. He may not have been planned, but he's still my son."

When he said it like that, every excuse in her mind sounded ridiculous. How could she explain that she didn't want Jared to grow up spoiled, rich but unloved? That she wanted him with her, not at some expensive boarding school? That she didn't want him to become a successful, miserable shell of a man like his father? All those excuses resulted from her primary fear that she couldn't shake. "I was afraid I would lose him."

Gavin's jaw still flexed with pent-up emotions. "You thought I would take him from you?"

"Wouldn't you?" Her gaze fixed on him, a challenge in her eyes. "Wouldn't you have swooped in the minute he was born and claimed him as your own? I'm sure your fancy friends and family would be horrified that a person like me was raising the future Brooks Express Shipping heir. It wouldn't be hard to deem me an unfit mother and have some judge from your father's social club grant you full custody."

"I wouldn't have done that."

"I'm sure you only would've done what you thought was best for your son, but how was I to know what that would entail? What would happen if you decided he would be better off with you and I was just a complication? I wouldn't have enough money or connections to fight you. I couldn't risk it." Sabine felt the tears prickling her eyes, but she refused to cry in front of Gavin.

"I couldn't bear the thought of you handing him off to nannies and tutors. Buying his affection with expensive gifts because you were too busy building the family company to spend time with him. Shipping him off to some boarding school as soon as he was old enough, under the guise of getting him the best education when you really just want him out of your hair. Jared wasn't planned. He wasn't the golden child of your socially acceptable marriage. You might want him on principle, but I couldn't be certain you would love him."

Gavin sat silent for a moment, listening to her tirade. The anger seemed to have run its course. Now he just looked emotionally spent, his dark eyes tired. He looked just like Jared after a long day without a nap.

Sabine wanted to brush the dark strands of hair from his weary eyes and press her palm against the rough stubble of his cheek. She knew exactly how it would feel. Exactly how his skin would smell…an intoxicating mixture of soap, leather and male. But she wouldn't. Her attraction to Gavin was a hurdle she had to overcome to leave him the first time. The years hadn't dulled her reaction to him. Now, it would be an even larger complication she didn't need.

"I don't understand why you would think that," he said at last, his words quieter now.

"Because that's what happened to you, Gavin." She lowered her voice to a soft, conversational tone. "And it's the only way you know how to raise a child. Nannies and boarding schools are normal to you. You told me yourself how your parents were always too busy for you and your siblings. How your house cycled through nannies like some people went through tissue paper. Do you remember telling me about how miserable and lonely you were when they sent you away to school? Why would I want that for Jared? Even if it came with all the money and luxury in the world? I wasn't about to hand him over to you so he could live the same hollow life you had. I didn't want him to be groomed to be the next CEO of Brooks Express Shipping."

"What's wrong with that?" Gavin challenged with a light of anger returning to the chocolate depths of his eyes. "There are worse things than growing up wealthy and becoming the head of a Fortune 500 company founded by your great-great-grandfather. Like growing up poor. Living in a small apartment with second-hand clothes."

"His clothes aren't secondhand!" she declared, her blood rushing furiously through her veins. "They're not from Bloomingdale's, but they aren't rags, either. I know that to you we look like we live in squalor, but we don't. It's a small apartment, but it's in a quiet neighborhood near the park where he can play. He has food and toys and most importantly, all the love, stability and attention I can possibly give him. He's a happy, healthy child."

Sabine didn't want to get defensive, but she couldn't help it. She recognized the tone from back when they were dating. The people in his social circles were always quick to note her shabby-chic fashion sense and lack of experience with an overabundance of flatware. They declared it charming, but Sabine could see the mockery in their eyes. They never thought she was good enough for one of the Brooks men. She wasn't about to let Gavin tell her that the way she raised her child wasn't good enough, either.

"I have no doubt that you're doing a great job with Jared. But why would you make it so hard on yourself? You could have a nice place in Manhattan. You could send him to one of the best private preschools in the city. I could get you a nice car and someone to help you cook and clean and take care of all the little things. I would've made sure you both had everything you needed—and *without* taking him from you. There was no reason to sacrifice those comforts."

"I didn't sacrifice anything," Sabine insisted. She knew those creature comforts came with strings. She'd rather do without. "I never had those things to begin with."

"No sacrifices?" Gavin shifted in the car to face her

directly. "What about your painting? I've kept an eye out over the years and haven't noticed any showings of your work. I didn't see any supplies or canvases lying around the apartment, either. I assume your studio space gave way to Jared's things, so where did all that go?"

Sabine swallowed hard. He had her there. She'd moved to New York to follow her dream of becoming a painter. She had lived and breathed her art every moment of the day she could. Her work had even met with some moderate success. She'd had a gallery showing and sold a few pieces, but it wasn't enough to live on. And it certainly wasn't enough to raise a child on. So her priorities shifted. Children took time. And energy. And money. At the end of the day, the painting had fallen to the bottom of her list. Some days she missed the creative release of her work, but she didn't regret setting it aside.

"It's in the closet," she admitted with a frown.

"And when was the last time you painted?"

"Saturday," she replied a touch too quickly.

Gavin narrowed his gaze at her.

"Okay, it was finger paints," Sabine confessed. She turned away from Gavin's heavy stare and focused on the yoga mat in her lap. He saw more than she wanted him to. He always had. "But," she continued, "Jared and I had a great time doing it, even if it wasn't gallery-quality work. He's the most important thing in the world to me, now. More important than painting."

"You shouldn't have to give up one thing you love for another."

"Life is about compromises, Gavin. Certainly you know what it's like to set aside what you love to do for what you're obligated to do."

He stiffened in the seat beside her. It seemed they

were both guilty of putting their dreams on the back burner, although for very different reasons. Sabine had a child to raise. Gavin had family expectations to uphold and a shipping empire to run. The tight collar of his obligations had chafed back when they were dating. It had certainly rubbed him bloody and raw by now.

When he didn't respond, Sabine looked up. He was looking out the window, his thoughts as distant as his eyes.

It was surreal to be in the same car with Gavin after all this time. She could feel his gravitational pull on her when they were this close. Walking away from him the first time had been hard. They dated for about a month and a half, but every moment they spent together had been fiercely passionate. Not just sexual, either. They enjoyed everything to the fullest, from spicy ethnic foods to political debates, museum strolls to making love under the stars. They could talk for hours.

Their connection was almost enough to make her forget they wanted different things from life. And as much as he seemed enticed by the exoticness of their differences, she knew it wouldn't last long. The novelty would wear off and they would either break up, or he would expect her to change for him. That was one thing she simply wouldn't do. She wouldn't conform for her parents and the small-minded Nebraska town she grew up in, and she wouldn't do it for him. She came to New York so she could be herself, not to lose her identity and become one of the Brooks Wives. They were like Stepfords with penthouse apartments.

She had briefly met some of Gavin's family, and it had scared the hell out of her. They hadn't been dating very long when they ran into his parents at a restaurant. It was an awkward encounter that came too early in the relationship, but the impact on Sabine had been huge. His mother was a flawless, polished accessory of his father's arm. Sabine was fairly certain that even if she wanted to be, she would be neither flawless nor polished. She didn't want to fade into the background of her own life.

It didn't matter how much she loved Gavin. And she did. But she loved herself more. And she loved Jared more.

But breathing the same air as Gavin again made her resolve weaken. She had neglected her physical needs for too long and made herself vulnerable. "So what do we do now?" Sabine asked at last.

As if he'd read her thoughts, Gavin reached over to her and took her hand in his. The warmth of him enveloped her, a tingle of awareness prickling at the nape of her neck. It traveled like a gentle waterfall down her back, lighting every nerve. Her whole body seemed to be awakening from a long sleep like a princess in a fairy tale. And all it had taken was his touch. She couldn't imagine what would happen if the dashing prince actually kissed her.

Kissed her? Was she insane? He was no dashing prince, and she had run from this relationship for a good reason. He may have tracked her down and she might be obligated to allow him to have a place in Jared's life, but that didn't mean they had to pick up where they left off. Quite the contrary. She needed to keep her distance from Gavin if she knew what was good for her. He'd let her go once, proving just how much she didn't matter to him. Anything he said or did now to the contrary was because of Jared. Not her.

His thumb gently stroked the back of her hand. Her

body remembered that touch and everything it could lead to. Everything she'd denied herself since she became a mother…

He looked up at her, an expression of grave seriousness on his face. "We get married."

Gavin had never proposed to a woman before. Well, it wasn't really even a proposal since he hadn't technically asked. And even though it wasn't candlelight and diamonds, he certainly never imagined a response like this.

Sabine laughed at him. Loudly. Heartily. For an unnecessarily long period of time. She obviously had no idea how hard it had been for him to do this. How many doubts he had to set aside to ask *anyone* to be a permanent part of his life, much less someone with a track record of walking away from him.

He'd thought they were having a moment. Her glossy lips had parted softly and her pale eyes darkened when he'd touched her. It should've been the right time, the perfect moment. But he'd miscalculated. Her response to his proposal had proved as much.

"I'm serious!" he shouted over her peals of laughter, but it only made her giggle harder. Gavin sat back in his seat and waited for her to stop. It took a few minutes longer than his pride would've liked. Eventually, she quieted and wiped her damp eyes with her fingertips.

"Marry me, Sabine," he said.

"No."

He almost wished Sabine had gone back to laughing. The firm, sober rejection was worse. It reminded him of her pained, resolved expression as she broke off their relationship and walked out of his life.

"Why not?" He couldn't keep the insulted tone from

his voice. He was a great catch. She should be thrilled to get this proposal, even as spur of the moment and half-assed as it was.

Sabine smiled and patted his hand reassuringly. "Because you don't want to marry me, Gavin. You want to do the right thing and provide a stable home for your son. And that's noble. Really. I appreciate the sentiment. But I'm not going to marry someone that doesn't love me."

"We have a child together."

"That's not good enough for me."

Gavin scoffed. "Making our son legitimate isn't a good enough reason for you?"

"We're not talking about the succession to the throne of England, Gavin. It's not exactly the horrid stigma it used to be. Having you in his life is more than enough for me. That's all I want from you—quality time."

"Quality time?" Gavin frowned. Somehow legally binding themselves in marriage seemed an easier feat.

"Yes. If you're committed enough to your son to marry his mother when you don't love her, you should be committed enough to put in the time. I'm not going to introduce a 'dad' into his life just so you can work late and ignore him. He's better off without a dad than having one that doesn't make an effort. You can't miss T-ball games and birthday parties. You have to be there when you say you will. If you can't be there for him one hundred percent, don't bother."

Her words hit him hard. He didn't have bad parents, but he did have busy ones. Gavin knew how it felt to be the lowest item on someone's priority list. How many times had he sat alone on the marble staircase of his childhood home and waited for parents who never showed up? How many times had he scanned the crowd at school pageants and ball games looking for family that wasn't there?

He'd always sworn he wouldn't do that to his own children, but even after having seen his son, the idea of him wasn't quite a firm reality in Gavin's mind. He had only this primitive need to claim the child and its mother. To finally have someone in his life that couldn't walk away.

That's why he'd rushed out to Brooklyn without any sort of plan. But she was right. He didn't know what to do with a child. His reflex would be to hand him off to someone who did and focus on what he was good at—running his family business. He couldn't afford the distraction, especially so close to closing his latest business deal.

And that was exactly what she was afraid of.

She had good reason, too. He'd spent most of their relationship vacillating between ignoring her for work and ignoring work for her. He never found the balance. A child would compound the problem. Part of the reason Gavin hadn't seriously focused on settling down was because he knew his work priorities would interfere with family life. He kept waiting for the day when things at BXS would slow down enough for him to step back. But it never happened. His father hadn't stepped back until the day he handed the reins over to Gavin, and he'd missed his children growing up to do it.

Gavin didn't have a choice any longer. He had a child. He would have to find a way—a better way than his father chose—to keep the company on top and keep his promises to his son and Sabine. He wasn't sure how the hell he would do it, but he would make it happen.

"If I put in the quality time, will you let me help you?"

"Help me with what?"

"With life, Sabine. If you won't marry me, let me get you a nice apartment in the city. Wherever you want to live. Let me help pay for Jared's education. We can enroll him in the best preschool. I can get someone to help around the house. Someone that can cook and clean, even pick up Jared from school if you want to keep working."

"And why would you want to do that? What you're suggesting is incredibly expensive."

"Maybe, but it's worth it to me. It's an investment in my child. Making your life easier will make you a happier, more relaxed mother to our son. He can spend more time playing and learning than sitting on the subway. And admittedly, having you in Manhattan will make it easier for me to see Jared more often."

He could see the conflict in Sabine's pale green eyes. She was struggling. She was proud and wouldn't admit it, but raising Jared on her own had to be difficult. Kids weren't cheap. They took time and money and effort. She'd already sacrificed her art. But convincing her to accept his offering would take time.

He knew Sabine better than she wanted to admit. She didn't want to be seen as one of those women who moved up in social status by calculated breeding. Jared had been an accident, of that he was certain. Judging by the expression on Sabine's face when she opened the door to her apartment, she would've rather had any man's son but his.

"Let's take this one step at a time, please," Sabine said, echoing his thoughts. There was a pained expression on her face that made him think there was more than just pride holding her back.

"What do you mean?"

"You've gone from having no kids to having a toddler and very nearly a fiancée in two hours' time. That's a big change for you, and for both Jared and me. Let's not uproot our lives so quickly." She sighed and gripped his hand. "Let's get the DNA results in, so there are no questions or doubts. Then we can introduce the idea of you to Jared and tell our families. From there, maybe we move into the city to be closer to you. But let's make these decisions over weeks and months, not minutes."

She glanced down at the screen on her cell phone. "I've got to get inside and set up."

"Okay." Gavin got out of the car and came around to open her door and help her out.

"I have tomorrow off. If you can make an appointment for DNA testing, call or text me and we'll meet you there. My number is the same. Do you still have it?"

He did. He'd very nearly dialed it about a hundred times in the weeks after she'd left. He'd been too proud to go through with the call. A hundred people had drifted in and out of his life, but Sabine leaving had caught him by surprise and it stung. He'd wanted to fight, wanted to call her and convince her she was wrong about them. But she wanted to go and he let her.

Now he could kick himself for not manning up and telling her he wanted her and didn't care what others thought about it. That he would make the time for her. Maybe then he would've been there to hear his son's heartbeat in the doctor's office, his first cries and his first words. Maybe then the mother of his child wouldn't look at him with wary eyes and laugh off his proposal of marriage like a joke.

He made a point of pulling out his phone and confirming it so she wouldn't think he knew for certain. "I do."

Sabine nodded and slowly started walking backward across the grass. Even after all this time apart, it felt awkward to part like strangers without a hug or a kiss goodbye. They were bonded for a lifetime now, and yet he had never felt as distant from her as he did when she backed away.

"I'll see you tomorrow, then," she said.

"Tomorrow," he repeated.

He watched as she regarded him for a moment at a distance. There was a sadness in her expression that he didn't like. The Sabine he remembered was a vibrant artist with a lust for life and experience. She had jerked him out of his blah corporate existence, demanded he live his life, not just go through the motions. Sabine was nothing like what he was supposed to have but absolutely everything he needed. He'd regretted every day since she'd walked out of his life.

Now, he regretted it more than ever, and not just because of his son. The sad, weary woman walking away from him was just a shadow of the person he once knew. And he hated that.

The outdoor lights kicked on, lighting the shimmer of tears in her eyes. "I'm sorry, Gavin," she said before spinning on her heels and disappearing through the doors of the community center.

She was sorry. And so was he.

Three

Gavin arrived at the office the next morning before seven. The halls were dark and quiet as he traveled to the executive floor of the BXS offices. The large corner office had once belonged to his father and his grandfather before him. Gavin's original office was down the hallway. He'd gotten the space when he was sixteen and started learning the business and then passed it along to his younger brother, Alan, when Gavin took over as CEO.

Opening the door, he walked across the antique rug and set his laptop bag and breakfast on the large wooden desk. The heavy mahogany furniture was originally from his great-grandfather's office and was moved here when BXS upgraded their location from the small building near the shipping yards.

His great-grandfather had started the company in

1930, Depression be damned. What began as a local delivery service expanded to trains and trucks and eventually to planes that could deliver packages all over the world. The eldest Brooks son had run the company since the day it opened. Everything about Brooks Express Shipping had an air of tradition and history that made it one of the most trusted businesses in America.

Frankly, it was a bit stifling.

Despite how he'd argued to the contrary with Sabine last night, they both knew this wasn't what he wanted to do with his life. The Brooks name came with responsibilities. Gavin had been groomed from birth to one day run BXS. He'd had the best education, interned with the company, received his MBA from Harvard… Each milestone putting him one step closer to filling his father's shoes. Even if they were too tight.

Sabine had been right about some things. He had no doubt his family would assume Jared would one day be the corporate successor to his father. The difference would be that Gavin would make certain *his* son had a choice.

He settled in at his desk, firing up his computer. He immediately sent an email to his assistant, Marie, about setting up a lab appointment for their DNA testing. With it, he included a note that this was a confidential matter. No one, literally no one, was to know what was going on. He trusted Marie, but she was friendly and chatty with everyone, including his father, who she used to work for. Gavin had barely come to terms with this himself. He certainly wasn't ready for the world, and especially his family, to know what was going on.

Marie wouldn't be in until eight, but she had a corporate smartphone and a long train ride in to work. He was certain she'd have everything handled before she arrived.

That done, he turned to the steaming-hot cup of coffee and the bagel he picked up on his way in. The coffee shop on the ground floor of the building was open well before most people stumbled into BXS for the day. Gavin spread cream cheese on his toasted bagel as he watched his in-box fill with new messages. Most were unimportant, although one caught his eye.

It was from Roger Simpson, the owner of Exclusivity Jetliners.

The small, luxury jet company specialized in private transportation. Whether you were taking a few friends for a weekend in Paris, transporting your beloved poodle to your summer home or simply refused to fly coach, Exclusivity Jetliners was ready and waiting to help. At least for now.

Roger Simpson wanted to retire. The business had been his life, and he was ready to finally relax and enjoy the fruits of his labor. Unlike BXS, he didn't have a well-groomed heir to take his place at the head of the company. He had a son, Paul, but from the discussions Roger and Gavin had shared, Roger would rather sell the company than let his irresponsible son drive it into the ground.

Gavin quickly made it known that he was interested. He'd been eight years old when his father let him ride in the cockpit of one of their Airbus A310 freighters. He'd immediately been enamored with planes and flying. For his sixteenth birthday, his parents had acquiesced and got him flying lessons.

He'd even entertained the idea of joining the Air Force and becoming a fighter pilot. There, sadly, was where that dream had died a horrible death. His father had tolerated Gavin's "hobby," but he wouldn't allow his son to derail his career path for a silly dream.

Gavin swallowed the old taste of bitterness on the back of his tongue and tried to chase it with his coffee. His father had won that battle, but he wasn't in charge anymore. He clicked on the email from Roger and scanned over the message.

BXS was about to offer a new service that would push them ahead of their shipping competitors—concierge shipping. It would appeal to the elite BXS clientele. Ones who wanted their things handled carefully and expeditiously and were willing to pay for the privilege.

The fleet of small planes from Exclusivity Jetliners would be transformed into direct freight jets that would allow the rich art lover to see to it that their new Picasso bought at auction over the phone would arrive safely at their home the same day. It would allow the fashion designer to quickly transport a dozen priceless gowns to an Academy Award nominee while she filmed on set two thousand miles from Hollywood.

It was a risk, but if it worked, it would give Gavin something he'd been wanting his whole life—the chance to fly.

Sabine had encouraged him years ago to find a way to marry his obligations and his passions. It had seemed impossible at the time, but long after she was out of his life, her words had haunted him.

Just as her words had haunted him last night. He'd lain in bed for hours, his brain swirling with everything that had happened after he'd answered Clay's phone call. Sabine had always had the innate ability to cut through his crap. She called it like she saw it, as opposed to all the polite society types who danced around delicate subjects and gossiped behind your back.

She didn't see Gavin as a powerful CEO. The money and the privilege didn't register on her radar at all, and really it never had. After years of women chasing after him, Sabine was the first woman he was compelled to pursue. He'd spied her across an art gallery and instantly felt the urge to possess her. She had no idea who he was or how much he was worth at first, and when she did, she didn't care. He insisted on taking her out to nice dinners, but Sabine was more interested in making love and talking for hours in bed.

But she couldn't ignore their differences. They'd lasted as long as they had by staying inside the protective bubble of the bedroom, but he could tell it was getting harder for Sabine to overlook the huge, platinum gorilla in the room. She didn't see his power and riches as an asset. It was just one thing on a list of many that made her believe they didn't have a future together. She would rather keep her son a secret and struggle to make ends meet than to have Jared live the life Gavin had.

What had she said? *…You know what it's like to set aside what you love to do for what you're obligated to do.*

He did. Gavin had done it his whole life because of some misguided sense of duty. He could've walked away at any time. Joined the Air Force. Sacrificed his inheritance and what little relationship he had with his parents. But then what would happen to the company? His brother couldn't run it. Alan hadn't so much as sat down in his token office in months. Gavin wasn't even sure if he was in the country. His baby sister, Diana, had a freshly inked degree from Vassar and absolutely no experience. His father wouldn't come out of retirement. That meant Gavin ran BXS or a stranger did.

And no matter what, he couldn't let that happen. It was a family legacy. One of his earliest memories was of coming into this very office and visiting his grandfather. Papa Brooks would sit Gavin on his knee and tell him stories about how his great-grandfather had started the company. Tears of pride would gather in the old man's dark eyes. Gavin and his father might have their differences, but he wouldn't let his grandfather down. He'd been dead for four years now, but it didn't matter. BXS and its legacy was everything to Papa Brooks. Gavin wouldn't risk it to chase a pipe dream.

A chime sounded at his hip. Gavin reached down to his phone to find a text from Marie. She'd arranged for an appointment at 4:15 with his concierge physician on Park Avenue. Excellent.

He could've just copied the information into another window and included the location to send it to Sabine, but he found himself pressing the button to call her instead. It was a dangerous impulse that he wished he could ignore, but he wanted to hear her voice. He'd gone so long without it that he'd gladly take any excuse to hear it again. It wasn't until after the phone began to ring that he realized it was 7:30 in the morning. Sabine had always been a night owl and slept late.

"Hello?" she answered. Her voice was cheerful and not at all groggy.

"Sabine? It's Gavin. I'm sorry to call so early. Did I wake you?"

"Wake me?" Sabine laughed. "Oh, no. Jared is up with the chickens, no later than 6:00 a.m. every morning. I tease him that he's going to grow up to be a farmer like his granddaddy."

Gavin frowned for a moment before he realized she was talking about her own father. Sabine spoke very rarely of her parents. Last he'd heard they were both alive and well in Nebraska, but Sabine wasn't in contact with them. It made Gavin wonder if he wasn't the only one who didn't know about Jared.

"My assistant got us an appointment." Gavin read her the information so she could write it down, including the address of the doctor's office.

"Okay," she said. "We'll meet you there at a little before 4:15."

"I'll pick you up," he offered.

"No, we'll take the subway. Jared likes the train. There's a stop about a block from there, so it's not a problem at all."

Sabine was fiercely independent. Always had been. It had made him crazy when they were dating. She wouldn't let him do anything for her. He wanted to argue with her now, but he wouldn't. His afternoon schedule was pretty hectic, and he'd have to shuffle a few things around to drive out to Brooklyn and get them in time unless he sent a car. And yet, he wasn't ready to end the conversation, either.

"After the appointment," he said, "may I take you and Jared to an early dinner?"

"Um…" Sabine delayed her response. She was probably trying to come up with a reason why she couldn't, but was failing.

"A little quality time," he added with a smile, happily using her own words to get his way.

"Sure," she said, caving. "That would be nice."

"I'll see you this afternoon."

"Goodbye," Sabine said, disconnecting the call.

Gavin smiled as he glanced down at his phone. He was looking forward to his afternoon with Jared. And even though the rational side of his brain knew that he shouldn't, he was looking forward to seeing Sabine again, as well.

Sabine was surprised that it didn't take long at the doctor's office. The paperwork took more time than anything else. Gavin and Jared got their cheeks swabbed, and they were told the office would call with the lab results on Monday.

By four forty-five, they were standing on the sidewalk watching the traffic stack up on Park Avenue. Sabine secured Jared in the collapsible umbrella stroller she sometimes took into the city. It was too busy to let him walk, even though he was getting more independent and wanted to.

"What would you like to eat?" Gavin asked.

Sabine was pretty sure that the majority of places he was used to eating at were not equipped to feed a picky toddler. She glanced around, getting her bearings for where she was in the city. "I think there's a good burger place about two blocks from here."

Gavin's gaze narrowed at her. "A burger?"

She swallowed her laugh. "Let's wait until Jared is at least five before we take him to Le Cirque. They don't exactly have a kid's menu."

"I know."

Sabine shook her head and started walking toward the restaurant. Gavin moved quickly to fall into step beside her.

"You're used to taking people out to nice places and spending a lot of money for dinner. I suppose that's what people expect of you, but that's not how Jared and I roll. We'll probably all eat for less than what you normally pay for a bottle of wine. And that's fine by us. Right, Jared?"

The little boy smiled and gave a thumbs-up. He'd learned the gesture in day care a few weeks ago and since then, a lot of things had called for it. "Cheeburger!"

"See?" Sabine said, looking over to Gavin. "He's easy to impress."

The restaurant was already a little busy, but they were able to order and get their food before their toddler started to revolt. Sabine tried to keep her focus on Jared, making sure he was eating small bites and not getting ketchup everywhere. It was easier than looking at Gavin and trying to guess what he was thinking.

Things were still very up in the air between them. He was being nice to her. More polite than she expected, under the circumstances. But once the test results came back, Sabine was certain that things would start to change. Gavin had sworn he wasn't about to snatch her baby from her arms, but she was more concerned about it happening slowly. A new apartment in the city. A new school for Jared. New clothes. New toys. Even if he gave up the idea of marrying for their child's sake, things would change for her, too. He'd insist she stop working. He'd give her spending money. Suggest they just move in with him.

And when the time came that she decided to move out, she was certain he'd see to it that Jared stayed behind in the stable home they'd created for him there. She'd be unemployed and homeless with no money of her own to fight him for custody.

These were the thoughts that had kept her quiet throughout her pregnancy. The same fears that made her hide Jared from his father. And yet, she found herself smiling as she watched Jared and Gavin color on the kid's menu together. There was a hamburger with legs dancing on one side. Jared was scribbling green across the bun. Gavin was more cautious, making the meat brown and the cheese orange as he stayed between the lines.

That was Gavin for you. No matter what he did, he always stayed between the lines. He never got dirty. Or screwed up anything.

Opposites attracted, but they were polar to the point of near incompatibility. A lot of Sabine's clothes had paint splattered on them from her art. She embraced that life was messy. You had to eat a little dirt before you died. Gavin was polished. Tailored. You couldn't find a speck of dirt beneath his fingernails.

How had she ever thought that dating Gavin was a good idea?

Her eyes drifted over his sharp features and thick, dark hair. His broad shoulders and strong jaw. In truth, that was why she'd let herself indulge. Gavin was a handsome, commanding specimen of a man. Every inch of him, from his large hands attempting to clutch a tiny crayon, to his muscular but trim frame, radiated health and power. He was interesting and thoughtful. Honorable and loyal to a fault.

If she'd *had* to get pregnant, her instincts had sought out a superior male to help her propagate the species.

Somehow, even that most scientific of thoughts spoke straight to her core. Her appraisal of Gavin had shot up her pulse. She felt a flush rise to her cheeks and chest.

The heat spread throughout her body, focusing low in her belly. She closed her eyes, hoping to take a private moment to wish away her desire and regain control.

"Do you need to do anything else in the city before I take you back to your place?"

No such luck. Sabine's eyes flew open to see Gavin looking at her with a curious gaze. "You don't have to take us back," she snapped. She wasn't certain she could take being so close to him in the car. At least not at the moment. "We'll take the subway."

"No, I insist." Gavin paid the check and handed his crayon over to Jared.

"Gavin, you have a two-passenger roadster with no car seat. You can't drive us home."

He smiled and fished into his pocket, pulling out the ticket for the garage attendant. "Not today. Today I have a four-door Mercedes sedan…"

Sabine opened her mouth to reiterate the lack of car seat when Gavin continued, "…with a newly installed combination car seat that Jared can use until he's eighty-five pounds."

Her mouth snapped shut. He was determined to undermine any arguments she might make. Sure, it was harmless when it came to rides home from dinner, but what about when the decisions were important? Would Gavin find a way to make sure he got his way then, too? He'd always seemed to win when they were dating, so she wouldn't be surprised.

Tonight, Sabine didn't feel like arguing. She waited with Jared while Gavin had the attendant retrieve his car. Admittedly, it was nice to just sit in the soft leather seats and let Gavin worry about the stressful exodus of traffic into Brooklyn. No running down stairs to the train platforms…no crowded, B.O.-smelling subway cars…

And when he pulled up right in front of her building and parked, trimming several blocks from her walk, she said, "Thank you."

"For what?"

"Driving us home."

Gavin frowned slightly at her. "Of course I would drive you home. There's no need to thank me for that."

Sabine glanced over her shoulder and found Jared out cold in his new car seat. "I think he likes it," she said. She glanced at her watch. It was a little after seven. It was earlier than Jared usually went to bed, and he'd probably beat the sun to rise, but that was okay. If she could get him upstairs, change his Pull-Up and take off his shoes without waking him up, she'd consider it a victory.

They got out of the car. Sabine walked around to the other side, but Gavin had already scooped up the sleepy toddler in his arms. Without waking, Jared put his head on Gavin's shoulder and clung to his neck. Gavin gently ran his palm over the child's head, brushing back the baby-soft strands of his dark hair and resting his hand on Jared's back to keep him steady.

Sabine watched with a touch of tears distorting her vision. It was sweet watching the two of them, like carbon copies of one another. It was only their second day together and already she could see Jared warming up to Gavin.

Gavin carried Jared through the building and into her apartment after she unlocked the door. Sabine led the way down the hall to the bedroom. Flipping on the lights, they were greeted with calming mint-green walls, cream wainscoting and a mural of Winnie the Pooh characters she'd painted above the crib. Her double bed was an afterthought on the opposite wall.

She slipped off Jared's shoes. His soft cotton pants and T-shirt would be fine to sleep in. She gestured for Gavin to lay him on the crib mattress and made quick work of changing him.

Jared immediately curled into a ball, reaching out for his stuffed dinosaur and pulling it to his chest. Sabine covered him with his blanket. They slipped out quietly, the night-light kicking on as the overhead light went out.

Sabine pulled the door closed gently and made her way back into the living room. She expected Gavin to make noises about leaving, but instead he loitered, his eyes focused on a painting on the wall over the dining room table.

"I remember this one," Gavin said, his fists in his pants pockets.

Sabine looked up at the canvas and smiled. "You should. I was painting that one while we were dating."

The background of the painting was intricately layered with a muted palette of white, cream, ivory, off-white and ecru. The design was extremely structured and orderly. The variations of the pattern were really quite remarkable if you could differentiate the subtle color differences.

It was Gavin on canvas. And across it, splatters of purple, black and green paint. Disorder. Chaos. Color. That was Sabine. It was a striking juxtaposition. One that when it was complete, was the perfect illustration of why as a couple they made good art, but not good sense.

"You weren't finished with it when I saw it last. Some of this is new, like the blue crosses. What did you end up calling it?"

The pale blue crosses were actually plus signs. The final addition to the work after seeing her own unexpected plus sign on a pregnancy test. "Conception," she said.

Gavin looked back at the painting and turned his head to look at it from a new angle. "It's very nice. I like the colors. It's a much-needed pop against the beige."

Sabine smiled. He didn't see the symbolism of their relationship in it at all and that was okay. Art was only half about what she created. The other half was how others perceived and experienced her work.

He turned back to her, his face serious. "You are a really talented artist, Sabine."

The compliment made her squirm a little. She was always uncomfortable with praise. Frankly, she wasn't used to it after growing up with parents who didn't understand why their daughter danced to a different drummer. "It's okay," she said with a dismissive wave of her hand. "Not my best work."

Gavin frowned and closed the gap between them. He clasped her hand in his and pulled it to the red silk of his tie. "No," he insisted. "It's not just okay. You're not just okay."

Sabine tried to pull away, but he wasn't having it. He bent his knees until he was at her eye level and she couldn't avoid his gaze.

"You are a gifted painter," he insisted. "You were then and you certainly are now. I was always amazed at how you could create such wonderful and imaginative things from just a blank canvas. You have a great deal of skill, Sabine, whether you think so or not. I hope our son has the same eye for the beautiful things in life."

The words were hard enough to hear when they were

about her, but knowing he wished the same for their son was too much for her to take. Her parents hadn't wanted her to be a painter. It was frivolous. They'd wanted her to stay home and work on the farm, grow up and marry a farmer, and then raise a brood of tiny farmers. She was absolutely nothing like they wanted. And the day she left for New York, they said as much.

Before she could change her mind, Sabine threw herself against the wall of Gavin's chest and hugged him tight. He seemed surprised at first, but then he wrapped his strong arms around her and pulled her close. "Thank you," she whispered into his lapel.

It felt good to be in his arms, surrounded in his warmth and spicy cologne. Good to be appreciated for her work even when she hadn't lifted a brush in two years. Good to have someone believe in her, even if it was the same man who let her walk away from him. She would be happy with his professional admiration if nothing else.

And yet, with her head pressed to his chest, she could hear his heart racing. His muscles were tense as he held her. He was either extremely uncomfortable hugging her or there was more than just admiration there.

Sabine lifted her head and looked up at him. Her breath caught in her throat as her eyes met his. They glittered with what could only be desire. His jaw was tight, but unlike last night, he wasn't angry. He swallowed hard, the muscles in his throat working hard down the column of his neck. She recognized the signs in Gavin. She knew them well but thought she'd never see him look at her like that again.

The intensity of his gaze flipped a switch in her own body. As it had in the restaurant, heat pooled in her cheeks and then rushed through her veins to warm every inch of her. She couldn't help it. There had been few things as exquisite in her life as being made love to by Gavin. It had come as a huge surprise considering how tightly buttoned-up he was, but there was no denying he knew just how to touch her. It was probably the worst thing she could do considering what was going on between them, but she wanted Gavin to touch her again.

He must have read it in her eyes because a moment later he dipped his head and brought his lips to hers. They were soft at first, molding to her mouth and drinking her in. Sabine gently pressed her hands against his chest, pushing up onto her toes to get closer to him.

His hands glided across her back, the heat of him penetrating through the fabric of her blouse and searing her skin. She wanted to feel those hands all over her body. It had been so long since someone had touched her that way. She didn't want it to stop. Not ever.

Sabine was about to lean in. She wanted to wrap her arms around his neck and press her body tight against his. As if he sensed the move, Gavin started to retreat. She could feel him pulling away, the cool air rushing between them and bringing with it reality. She pulled away, too, wrapping her arms across her chest to ward off the chill and its evidence on her aching body.

Gavin looked down at her and cleared his throat. "I'd better go."

Sabine nodded and moved slowly with him toward the door.

"Good night, Sabine," he said in a hoarse whisper. He took a step back, straightening his suit coat, and then gripped the brass knob in his hand.

"Good night," she whispered, bringing her fingers up to gently touch her lips. They were still tingling with his kiss as he vanished through her doorway. "Good night."

Four

"We have a date this afternoon. I mean a playdate. I mean, aw hell, I have no idea what's going on," Sabine lamented. She was folding a stack of shirts and paused with one clutched to her chest. "You know, a few days ago I was living my life like a criminal on the run, but I felt like I had a better grip on things."

Adrienne smiled at her and turned to change the outfit on the mannequin by the wall. "It's a big change," she said. "But so far, it's not a bad change, right?"

"That's true. I guess that's what worries me. I keep waiting for the other shoe to drop."

The boutique was open, but the foot traffic usually didn't pick up until closer to lunchtime on a Saturday. At the moment, Sabine and Adrienne were alone in the store and able to speak freely about the dramatic turn of events in her life. Normally, Sabine ran the shop alone until another employee, Jill, came in later in the day. Today, Adrienne came in as well to relieve Sabine so she could meet Gavin.

"I don't think he's going to steal Jared away from you, Sabine. It sounds like he's been pretty reasonable so far."

"I know," she said, folding the last shirt and adding it to the neat display. "But he doesn't have the DNA results back yet and won't until Monday. If he was going to make a move, it wouldn't be until he had the advantage. The Gavin I knew three years ago was…calculating and ruthless. He had absolutely no qualms about sitting back and waiting for the perfect moment to strike."

"This isn't a business deal and he's not a cobra. You two have a child together. It's different." Adrienne pulled out a pin and fitted the top of the dress to the form.

Sabine stopped and admired the outfit Adrienne had designed. The sexy sheath dress was fitted with a square neckline, but it had fun details like pockets and a bright print to make it pop. It was perfect for the summer with some strappy heels or colorful ballet flats. She'd been tempted to use her employee discount to buy it for herself, but there wasn't much point. That was the kind of dress a woman wanted to wear on a date or a night out with the girls. She hadn't had either in a very long time. And despite Gavin proposing one night and kissing her the next, she didn't think her Facebook relationship status would be changing anytime soon.

"Work and life are the same to Gavin. I mean, he didn't propose to me. Not really. It was more like an offer to buy out my company. A business merger. Just what a girl wants to hear, right?"

Adrienne turned and looked at Sabine with her hands planted on her hips. "And the kiss?"

The kiss. The one thing that didn't make sense. She knew he was her Achilles' heel so it didn't surprise her that she fell into his arms, but his motives were sketchy. "Strategy. He knows my weakness where he's concerned. He's just buttering up the competition to get his way."

"You really think that's all it was?" Her boss looked unconvinced.

Sabine flopped down onto an upholstered bench outside the changing rooms. "I don't know. It didn't feel like strategy. It felt…" Her mind drifted back to the way her body had responded to his touch. The way her lips tingled long after he'd left. She sighed and shook her head. "It doesn't matter what it felt like. The fact of the matter is that Gavin doesn't love me. He never has. His only interest in me back then was as a source of rebellion against his uptight family. Now, I'm nothing more than a vehicle to his son. And when he gets tired of the games, he'll remove the obstacle—*me*."

"You don't think he's interested in a relationship with you?" Adrienne sat down beside her.

"Why would he be? He wasn't interested the last time. At least not enough to so much as blink when it ended. I mean, I thought there was more between us than just sex, but he was always so closed off. I had no idea how he really felt, but when he let me walk out the door like I was nothing more than an amusement to occupy his time…I knew I was replaceable. Gavin never would've sought me out if it wasn't for Jared."

"You broke up with him," Adrienne reminded her. "Maybe his pride kept him from chasing after you. Listen, I'm married to one of those guys. They're all about running their little empires. They're the king of their own kingdoms. In the business world, showing weakness is like throwing chum in the ocean—the sharks start circling. They keep it all inside for so long that after a while, they lose touch with their own sense of vulnerability."

Her boss knew what she was talking about. Adrienne's husband was Will Taylor, owner of one of the oldest and most successful newspapers in New York. He came from a long line of CEOs, just as Gavin had. Even then, she'd seen Adrienne and Will together multiple times, and he was putty in her hands. And happily so. Will at work and Will at home were completely different people.

But somehow Sabine had a hard time picturing Gavin with a marshmallow center beneath his hard candy shell. They'd shared some intimate moments together while they'd dated, but there was always an element of control on his part. They were together only a short time, but it was an intense relationship. She gave so much and yet he held back from her. She had no way of knowing the parts he kept hidden, but more than likely, it was his apathy. "You're saying he let me walk away and cried himself to sleep that night?"

Adrienne chuckled. "Well, maybe that's taking it a little far. But he might have had regrets and didn't know what to do about it. Jared gives him a good reason to see you again without having to address any of those icky, uncomfortable feelings."

A pair of ladies came into the shop, so they put their conversation on hold for now. While the women looked around, Sabine moved over to the checkout counter and crouched down to inventory the stock of pink boutique bags with Adrienne's signature across the side. The passive activity helped her think.

Feelings were definitely not Gavin's forte. Or at least sharing them. She was certain he had them, he just bottled them up on the inside. But feelings for her? She doubted that.

Gavin might be attracted to her. The kiss they shared might've been him testing the waters of resuming a physical relationship. They'd always had an undeniable chemistry. She knew the minute she saw him the first time that she was in trouble. It was at a gallery showing for a local contemporary artist. Sabine had gotten lost in the lines and colors of one of the pieces and the rest of the world disappeared.

At least until she heard the low rumble of a man's voice in her ear. "It looks like an expensive mistake to me."

She'd turned in surprise and nearly choked on a sip of champagne when she saw him. He wasn't at all the kind of man she was used to. He wore an expensive suit and a watch that cost more money than she'd made in the past year. Men like Gavin typically turned their nose up at Sabine. But he'd looked at her with dark eyes that twinkled with amusement and desire.

Her pulse had shot up, her knees melted to butter beneath her, and she'd found herself without a witty response. Just that quickly, she was lost.

The weeks that followed were some of the greatest of her life. But not once in that time had he ever looked at her with anything more than lust. So as much as she'd like to think Adrienne was right, she knew better. He'd either been using their attraction to his advantage or using their situation to get laid.

One of the ladies tried on a blouse and then bought it, along with a scarf. Sabine rang her up and they left the store. The chime of the door signaled that her conversation with Adrienne could resume.

"So where are you guys going on your playdate today?" Adrienne called from the stockroom.

"We're going to the Central Park Zoo."

"That should be fun," Adrienne said, returning to the front with her arms full of one of her newest dress designs. "Was that his idea?"

"No," Sabine chuckled. She reached out to take several of the outfits from her. "He didn't have a clue of what to do with a two-year-old. I suggested the zoo because I wanted us to do something that didn't involve a lot of money."

Adrienne wrinkled her delicate nose. "What do you mean?"

They carried the dresses over to the empty rack and organized them by size. "I don't want Gavin buying Jared anything yet. At least not big, expensive things. He used to tell me that his father only ever took him shopping. I can't keep him from buying things forever, but that's not how I want to start off."

"Money isn't a bad thing, Sabine. I never had it until I married Will, and trust me, it takes some adjusting to get used to having a lot of it. But it can be used for good, too, not just for evil."

"It's also not a substitute for love or attention. I want Gavin to really try. Right now, Jared is still young, but before too long, he's going to be in the 'gimme' stage. I don't want Gavin buying affection with expensive gifts."

"Try to keep an open mind," Adrienne suggested. "Just because he buys Jared something doesn't mean he isn't trying. If getting him a balloon makes Jared smile, don't read too much into it. Just enjoy your afternoon." Adrienne stopped and crinkled her nose, making a funny face at Sabine.

"What's the matter?"

"I don't know. My stomach is a little upset all of a sudden. I think my smoothie is turning on me. Either that, or I'm nauseated by all your drama."

Sabine laughed. "I'm sorry my crazy life is making you ill. I've got some antacids in my purse if you need them."

"I'll be fine," Adrienne insisted. She looked down at her watch. "You'd better get going if you're going to meet him on time. Worry about having fun instead."

Sabine nodded. "Okay," she said. "We will have a good time, I promise."

She hoped she was right.

As Gavin stepped out of his apartment building onto Central Park South and crossed the street, he realized just how long it had been since he'd actually set foot in Central Park. He looked out at it every day but never paid any attention to the looming green hulk that sprawled out in front of him.

His first clue was that he was a little overdressed for a summer afternoon at the zoo. He'd left the tie at home, but he probably could've forgone the suit coat, too. A pair of jeans or khakis and a polo shirt would've suited just fine. He considered running his jacket back upstairs, but he didn't want to be late.

When he was younger, he'd enjoyed jogging along the paths or hanging out and playing Frisbee with friends in the Sheep Meadow. The more involved he got in the management of BXS, the less important trees and sunshine seemed in his agenda. He and Sabine had taken a horse-drawn carriage through the park one evening when they were dating, but the closest he had gotten to it since then was a gala at the Met last year.

By the time he reached the front entrance to the zoo, he could feel the sweat forming along his spine. He slipped out of the jacket and threw it over his arm after rolling up his sleeves. It helped, but not much. He was supposed to meet Sabine and Gavin just outside the brick archways that marked the entrance, but he didn't see them anywhere.

He unclipped his phone from his belt to look at the time. He was a few minutes early. He opted to flip through some emails. He'd hit a little bit of a snag with the Exclusivity Jetliners merger. The owner's son, Paul, had found out about his father's plans and was throwing a fit. Apparently he wasn't pleased about watching his inheritance getting sold off. Gavin was paying a pretty penny for the company, but Roger's son seemed to fancy playing CEO. Roger was starting to second-guess the sale.

He fired off a couple quick emails, but his attention was piqued by the sound of a child's laughter in the distance. It was one of those contagious giggles that made you smile just to hear it. He looked up in the direction of the sound and saw Sabine and Jared playing in the shade of a large tree.

Slipping his cell phone back in the holster, he made his way over to where they were. Sabine was crouched down beside Jared, dressed in capris and a tank top. Her dark hair was pulled back into a ponytail and a bright red backpack was slung over her shoulders.

Jared was playing with another one of his trucks. In the mud. Apparently, the kid had managed to find the only mud bog in the park. He was crouched barefoot in the brown muck, ramming his trucks through the sludge. He made loud truck noises with his mouth and then giggled hysterically when the mud splashed up onto his shirt. He was head-to-toe filthy and happy as a little piglet.

Gavin's instinct was to grab Jared and get him out of the dirt immediately. There had to be a restroom somewhere nearby where they could rinse him off. But then he saw the smile on Sabine's face. She wasn't even remotely concerned about what Jared was doing.

His mother would've had a fit if she had found him playing in the mud. His nanny would've had to hose him off outside and then thoroughly scrub him in the tub. When he was dry, he would've been given a lengthy lecture about how getting dirty was inappropriate and his nanny would've been fired for not keeping a better eye on him.

Jared dropped one of the trucks in the puddle and the water splashed up, splattering both him and Sabine. Gavin expected her to get upset since she'd gotten dirty now, but she just laughed and wiped the smear of muddy water off her arm. It was amazing. It made Gavin want to get dirty, too.

"Oh, hey," Sabine said, looking up to see him standing nearby. She glanced at her watch. "I'm sorry to keep you waiting. We got here a little early and Jared can't pass up some good mud." She stood up and whipped the backpack off her shoulders.

"Not a problem," he said as he watched her pull out

an assortment of things including wet wipes, a large, plastic zip bag and a clean shirt.

"All right, buddy," she said. "Time to go to the zoo with Gavin. Are you ready?"

"Yeah!" Jared said, immediately perking up at the suggestion of a new adventure.

"Give me your trucks first." She put all the muddy toys in the bag and then used his dirty shirt to wipe up a good bit of the muck off his hands and feet before shoving it in there, as well. The baby wipes made quick work of the rest, then the clean shirt and the little socks and sneakers she'd taken off went back on. "Good job!" she praised, giving him a tiny high five and zipping up the backpack.

Gavin was amazed by the process. Not only did she let Jared get dirty, she was fully prepared for the eventuality. He'd always just thought of Sabine as the artistic type. She was laid-back and went with the flow as he expected, but she also had a meticulous bit of planning underneath it all that he appreciated. She had the motherhood thing down. It was very impressive.

"We're ready," she said, bending down to pick Jared up.

Gavin had to smile when he noticed the speck of mud on Sabine's cheek. "Not quite yet," he said. Without thinking, he reached out to her, running the pad of his thumb across her cheekbone and wiping it away. The moment he touched her, he sensed a change in the energy between them. Her pale green eyes widened, the irises darkening in the center to the deep hunter green he remembered from their lovemaking. A soft gasp of surprise escaped her glossy pink lips.

His body reacted, as well. The touch brought on the

familiar tingle that settled between his shoulder blades and sent a shot of pure need down his spine. He wanted Sabine. There was no use in denying it. There was something about her that spoke to his most base instincts. Their time apart hadn't changed or dulled the attraction. In fact, it seemed to have amplified it.

That night at her apartment, he had to kiss her. There was no way he could walk out of there without tasting her again. Once he did, he could feel the floodgates giving way. He had to leave. And right then. If he had lingered a moment longer, he wouldn't have been able to stop himself.

Their relationship was complicated. There were a lot of proverbial balls still in the air. He wasn't dumb enough to get emotionally involved with Sabine again, but leaping back into a physical relationship with her, at least this soon, was a bad idea, too. For now, he needed to try and keep his distance on both fronts.

Why, then, was he standing in the middle of Central Park cradling Sabine's face with a throbbing erection? Because he was a masochist.

"A…uh…stray bit of Jared's handiwork," he said. He let his hand drop back to his side before he did something stupid in public. Instead, he turned to look at Jared. "Are you ready to see the monkeys?"

"Yeah!" he cheered, clapping his chubby hands together.

They bought their tickets and headed inside. Starting at the sea lion pool, they made their way around to visit the penguins and the snow leopards. He enjoyed watching his son's eyes light up when he saw the animals.

"Do you guys come here a lot?" he asked, leaning on

the railing outside the snow monkey exhibit. "He really seems to like it."

"We actually haven't been here before. I was waiting until he was a little older. This seemed like the perfect opportunity."

Gavin was surprised. Somehow he'd thought he had missed all his son's firsts, but there were more to be had than he expected. "I've never been here, either."

Sabine looked at him with disbelief lining her brow. "You've lived in New York your whole life and you've never been to the zoo?"

"Saying I lived here my whole life isn't entirely accurate. My family lived here, but I was gone off to school a lot of the time."

"So not even as a child? Your nannies never brought you here?"

"Nope. Sometimes we came to the park to play or walk, but never to the zoo. I'm not sure why. My boarding school took a field trip to Washington, D.C., once. We went to the Smithsonian and the National Zoo on that trip. I think I was fourteen or so. But I've never had the chance to come here."

"Have you ever been to a petting zoo?"

At that, Gavin had to laugh. "A petting zoo? Absolutely not. My mother would have a fit at the thought of me touching dirty animals. I never even had pets as a kid."

Sabine wrinkled her nose at him. "Well, then, today is your day. We'll head over to the children's zoo after this and you and Jared can both pet your first goat."

A goat? He wasn't so sure that he was interested in that. Sabine seemed to sense his hesitation. "Maybe we can start you off slow. You can hold a rabbit. They have places to wash your hands. I also have hand sanitizer in my bag. You'll be okay, I promise."

Gavin chuckled at Sabine. She was mothering him just the same as she did to coax Jared into trying something new. He wasn't used to that.

They were on their way to the children's zoo when he felt his cell phone buzzing at his hip. He looked down at the screen. It was Roger. He had to take this call.

"Excuse me one minute," he said.

Sabine frowned but nodded. "I'll take Jared to the restroom while we're waiting."

Gavin answered the phone and spent the next ten minutes soothing Roger's concerns. He didn't want this opportunity to slip through his fingers. Acquiring those private jets was as close to fulfilling his childhood dream as he might ever get. He had a plane of his own, but it was small and didn't have anywhere near the range of Roger's jets. He longed for the day when he could pilot one of those planes to some far-off destination. He was a falcon on a tether now. He wanted to fly free, and he wasn't going to let Paul Simpson's desire to play at CEO ruin it.

It was going well so far. He was able to address all of Roger's concerns. Things might be back on track if he could keep the owner focused on what was best for his family and his company. But it was taking some time. The conversation was still going when Sabine returned. She didn't seem pleased.

He covered the receiver with his hand. "I'm almost done. I can walk and talk," he said.

She turned and started walking away with Jared. He followed close behind them, but he was admittedly distracted. By the time he finally hung up, Gavin had already missed out on feeding the ducks. Jared was quacking and clumsily chasing one at the moment.

Sabine was watching him play with a twinkle in her eye. She loved their son so much. He could tell that Jared was everything to her. He appreciated that about her. His parents had never been abusive or cruel, but they had been distant. Busy. They weren't hands-on at all. Jared hadn't had all the privileges that Gavin grew up with, but he did have a loving, doting mother.

Who was frowning intently at Gavin.

"I'm sorry," he said. "It was important."

She shook her head and turned back to look at Jared. One of the zoo employees was holding a rabbit so he could pet it. "That's the most important thing, right there, Gavin."

Jared turned around and grinned at his mother with such joy it made Gavin's chest hurt. "A bunny," he exclaimed, hopping around on his little legs like a rabbit.

She was right. He needed to be in this 100 percent. Jared deserved it. And so did Sabine.

Five

There was a knock on the door early Sunday morning. Sabine was making pancakes while Jared played with blocks on the floor. Sunday was their easy day. There was no work or preschool. They were both still in their pajamas and not expecting company.

She was surprised to find Gavin on her doorstep. She was even more surprised to find he was wearing jeans and a T-shirt. It was a Gucci T-shirt, but at least it wasn't a suit. And it looked good on him. The black shirt fit his muscular frame like a second skin, reminding her of the body he hid beneath blazers and ties. And the jeans… they were snug in all the right places, making her mouth go dry in an instant.

He caught her so off guard, she didn't notice at first that he had a large canvas and a bag of painting supplies in his hands.

"Gavin," she said. "I wasn't expecting you this morning." After yesterday, she didn't figure she would see him until the test results came back. She could tell that he was trying yesterday, but his thoughts were being pulled in ten different directions. Even after he got off the phone, he was checking it constantly and replying to emails. He had a business to run.

And yet, here he was.

"I know. I wanted it to be a surprise."

Sabine wasn't big on surprises. With Gavin, it was more that he wanted to do something his way and to keep her from arguing, he wouldn't tell her until the last second. Surprise! But still, she was curious. "Come on in," she said.

Gavin stepped in, leaning the canvas against the bookcase. "Hey, big guy," he said to Jared. He got up from his blocks and came over to hug Gavin's leg. Gavin scooped the toddler up and held him over his head, and then they "soared" around the living room making airplane noises. Jared the Plane crash-landed onto the couch in a fit of giggles and tickling fingers poking at his tummy.

It had only been a few days, but she could tell that Jared was getting attached to Gavin. It was a good thing. She knew that. But still, she worried. He'd put in a decent effort so far, but could he keep it up for the next sixteen years? She wasn't sure. But she did know that he'd better not screw this up.

"I was making pancakes," she said, turning and heading back into the kitchen. "Have you had breakfast?"

"That depends," he said, pausing in the tickle fight. "What kind of pancakes are they?"

"Silver-dollar pancakes with blueberries."

"Nope." Gavin smiled. "I haven't had breakfast." He let Jared return to his blocks. "I'll be right back, big guy."

He followed her into the kitchen, leaning against the entryway. The kitchen was too small for both of them to be in there and get anything done. She tried to ignore his physical presence and how much of the room he took up without even entering, but she failed. The sight of him in those tight jeans was more than she could take. Her body instantly reacted to his nearness, her mouth going dry and her nipples pebbling against the thin fabric of her T-shirt.

She spun to face the stove before he could notice and decided to focus on pancakes, not the sexy man lurking nearby. Eyeing the batter, she decided she needed a larger batch to feed a man of his size. "So what brings you here this morning?"

Gavin watched her fold in another handful of dried blueberries. "I wanted to make up for yesterday."

Sabine tried not to react. She was happy that he was making the effort, but failing Jared and then making a grand gesture to appease his conscience was a dangerous cycle. She'd rather he just be present the first time. "How's that?"

"I saw in the paper that the Big Apple Circus is here. I got tickets for this afternoon."

Just as she'd thought. She had no problems with going to the circus, but he didn't ask her. He didn't call to see if that was something they might want to do. What if Jared was petrified of clowns? Or if they had other plans today? Gavin just bought the tickets and assumed that everything would go the way he'd planned.

But—he was trying, she reminded herself. "Jared

would probably enjoy that. What time do we need to leave for the show?"

"Well," Gavin said, "that's only part of the surprise. *We* aren't leaving. You're staying."

Sabine looked up from the griddle. "What do you mean?"

"I just got tickets for Jared and me. I thought you might enjoy an afternoon to yourself. I even brought you some painting supplies."

That explained the stuff he brought in with him. She'd been so thrown off by his unannounced arrival that she hadn't questioned it yet. She supposed that she should be excited and grateful, but instead, her stomach ached with worry. Gavin was taking her son someplace without her. She didn't really like the sound of that. He didn't know anything about children. What if Jared got sick? Or scared? Did Gavin even know that Jared wasn't fully potty trained yet? Just the idea of him changing dirty Pull-Ups started a rumble of nervous laughter in her chest that she fought down.

"I don't think that's a good idea," she managed to say.

Gavin's dark brow drew together in consternation. "Why not? You said you wanted me to be there. To be involved."

"It's been less than a week, Gavin. You've spent a couple hours with him, sure, but are you ready to take care of him on your own for a day?" Sabine turned back to the stove and flipped over the pancakes. She grabbed one of Jared's superhero plates and slid a couple tiny pancakes onto it beside the slices of banana she'd already cut up.

"You don't think I can handle it?"

She sighed heavily. Ignoring him, she poured some

blueberry syrup into the small bowl built into the dish and grabbed a sippy cup with milk from the refrigerator. She brushed past him to go into the living room. Jared had a tiny plastic table and chair where he could eat. She set down his breakfast and called him over. Once he was settled, she turned back to look at Gavin. He was still standing in the doorway to the kitchen looking handsome and irritated all at once.

"I don't know," she admitted. "I don't know if you can handle it or not. That's the problem. We don't really know one another that well."

Gavin crossed his arms over his chest and leaned against the door frame. His biceps bulged against the constraints of the shirt, drawing her eyes down to his strong forearms and rock-hard chest. It was easier to focus on that than the strangely cocky expression on his face.

"We know each other *very* well," he said with a wicked grin curling his lips.

Sabine approached him, stopping just short of touching him. "Your ability to give me an orgasm has no bearing on whether or not you can care for a toddler."

At the mention of the word *orgasm* his gaze narrowed at her. He swallowed hard but didn't reach for her. "I disagree. Both require an attention to detail. Anticipating what another person wants or needs. I don't think it matters if what they need is a drink, a toy or a mind-blowing physical release."

Mind-blowing. Sabine couldn't stop her tongue from gliding out over her lips. They'd gotten painfully dry. His gaze dropped to her mouth, then back to her eyes. There was a touch of amusement in his gaze. He knew he was getting to her.

"What if what they need is their poopy diaper changed? Or you gave them too much cotton candy and they spew blue muck all over the backseat of your Mercedes? Not quite as sexy."

The light of attraction in his eyes faded. It was hard to keep up the arousal with that kind of imagery. That's why she hadn't bothered dating in all this time. Maybe she should reconsider. She might not feel as vulnerable to Gavin's charms if she had an outlet that didn't involve him.

His expression hardened for a moment. He seemed irritated with her. "Stop trying to scare me away. I know taking care of a child isn't easy. It can be messy. But it's just a few hours to start. I can handle it. Will you let me do this for you? Please?"

"Do this for *me?* Shouldn't you be doing this for your son?"

"I am. Of course, I am. I want a relationship with Jared more than anything. But to do that, you have got to trust me. I will return him to you tonight, well fed, well cared for and, for the most part, clean. But you have to do your part. You have to let me try. Let me mess up. Enjoy your free afternoon. Paint something beautiful because you can. Go get a pedicure."

Sabine had to admit that sounded wonderful. She hadn't had an afternoon to herself since she went into labor. She didn't have any family here to watch Jared. She tried to only use Tina's services when she had to for classes. She hadn't had a day just to relax. And to paint…

She pushed past him into the kitchen to finish making pancakes. Gavin stayed in the doorway, allowing her the space to think, while also keeping an eye on Jared. She appreciated having someone to do that. She hadn't had another set of eyes to help before. Since Jared became mobile, she hadn't been able to shower, cook or do anything without constantly peeking out to check on him. Life was a little easier when he sat in his swing or bouncy chair while she did what needed to be done.

A whole afternoon?

She wanted to say yes, but she couldn't shake the worry. It was probably going to be fine. There was only so much trouble that could befall them in an afternoon at the circus. If Jared came home covered in blue vomit, the world wouldn't end. And it was a family-oriented event. She had no doubt that if another mother saw Gavin and Jared in a meltdown moment, she would step in to help.

Sabine finished the pancakes and turned off the burner. She slid a stack onto her plate and the other onto a plate for Gavin. Turning around, she offered one to him. When he reached for it, she pulled it back slightly.

"Okay," she said. "You can go. But I want you to text and check in with me. And if anything remotely worrisome happens—"

Gavin took the plate from her. "I will call you immediately. Okay?"

Sharing Jared with someone else was going to be hard, she could tell already. But it could be good, too. Two parents were double the hands, double the eyes, double the love. Right? "Okay, all right. You win. Just don't feed him too much sugar. You'll regret it."

Gavin couldn't remember being this tired, ever. Not when he was on the college rowing team. Not when he stayed up late studying for an exam. Not even after spending all night making love to a beautiful woman. How on earth did parents do this every day? How did

Sabine manage to care for Jared alone, work full-time, teach yoga…it was no wonder she'd stopped painting. He was bone-tired. Mentally exhausted.

And it was one of the best days of his life.

Seeing Jared's smile made everything worth it. That was what kept parents going. That moment his son's face lit up when he saw an elephant for the first time. Or the sound of his laughter when the clowns were up to their wacky antics.

The day hadn't been without its mishaps. Jared had dropped his ice cream and went into a full, five-alarm meltdown. Gavin knew Sabine didn't want him buying a bunch of things, but he gladly threw down the cash for the overpriced light-up sword to quiet him down. There was also a potty emergency that was timed just as they neared the front of the mile-long food line. Sabine had begun potty training recently and had told him that if Jared asked, they were to go, right then. So they did. And ended up at the end of the line, waiting another twenty minutes for hot dogs and popcorn.

But the world hadn't ended. There had been no tragedies, and he texted as much to Sabine every hour or so. The day had been filled with lights and sound and excitement. So much so that by the time they made it back to the apartment, Jared was out cold. Gavin knew exactly how he felt.

He carried the exhausted toddler inside, quietly tapping at the apartment door so as to not wake him up. When Sabine didn't answer, he tried the knob and found it unlocked. He expected to find Sabine frantically painting. This was her chance, after all, to indulge her suppressed creativity. Instead, she was curled up on the couch, asleep.

Gavin smiled. He had told her to spend the afternoon doing whatever she wanted. He should've guessed that a nap would be pretty high on the list. He tiptoed quietly through the living room and into the bedroom. Following the routine from Thursday night, he laid Jared in the crib and stripped him down into just his T-shirt and shorts. He covered him with the blanket and turned out the lights.

Sabine was still asleep when he came out. He knew he couldn't leave without waking her up, but he couldn't bear to disturb her. He eased down at the end of the couch and decided to just wait until she woke up.

He enjoyed watching Sabine sleep. She had always been one to work hard and play hard, so when she slept, it was a deep sleep and it came on quickly. There were many nights where he had lain in bed and just studied her face. Gavin had memorized every line and curve. He'd counted her eyelashes. There was just something about her that had fascinated him from the first moment he saw her.

The weeks they'd spent together were intense. He couldn't get enough of her. Sabine was a breath of fresh air to a man hanging from the gallows. She'd brought him back to life with her rebellious streak and quest for excitement. He'd loved everything about her, from her dazzling smile to her ever-changing rainbow-streaked hair. He'd loved how there was always a speck of paint somewhere on her body, even if he had to do a detailed search to find it. She was so different from every other woman he'd ever known.

For the first time, he'd allowed himself to start opening up to someone. He'd begun making plans for Sabine to be a permanent fixture in his life. He hadn't anticipated her bolting, and when she did, he shut down. Gavin hadn't allowed himself to realize just how much he'd missed her until this moment.

She didn't trust him. Not with her son and not with her heart. Gavin hadn't appreciated it when he had it—at least not outwardly. He never told her how he felt or shared his plans for their future. That was his own fault, and they missed their chance at love. But even with that lost, he wanted her back in his bed. He ached to run his fingers through her hair. Tonight, it was pulled up on top of her head, the silky black and bright purple strands jumbled together. He wanted to touch it and see it sprawled across the pillowcase.

His eyes traveled down her body to the thin shirt and shorts she was wearing. He didn't think it was possible, but she was more beautiful now than she had been back then. She wouldn't believe him if he told her that, but it was true. Motherhood had filled out some of the curves she'd lacked as a struggling artist. He remembered her getting so engrossed in her work that sometimes she would simply forget to eat. Gavin would come to the apartment with takeout and force her to take a break.

Now she had nicely rounded hips that called to him to reach out and glide his palms over them. He wanted to curl up behind her and press her soft body into his. He wanted to feel her lean, yoga-toned muscles flexing against him. The sight of her in that skimpy workout outfit had haunted him since that first night.

Her newly developed muscles didn't make up for the mental strain, however. Even in her sleep, a fine line ran between her eyebrows. She made a certain face when she was frustrated or confused, and that line was the result. There were faint circles under her eyes. She was worn out. He was determined to make things easier for her. No matter how their relationship ended or his feelings where she was concerned, she deserved the help he could provide.

She just had to let him.

"Gavin," Sabine whispered.

He looked up, expecting to see her eyes open, but she was talking in her sleep. Calling his name in her sleep. He held his breath, waiting to see if she spoke again.

"Please," she groaned, squirming slightly on the sofa. "Yes. I need you."

Gavin nearly choked on his own saliva. She wasn't just dreaming about him. She was having an erotic dream about him. The mere thought made his jeans uncomfortably tight.

"Touch me."

Gavin couldn't resist. He reached out and placed his hand on the firm curve of her calf. He loved the feel of her soft skin against him. It made his palm tingle and his blood hum in his veins. Just a simple touch. No other woman had had this effect on him. Whatever it was that drew them together was still here, and as strong as ever.

"Gavin?"

He looked up to see Sabine squinting at him in confusion. She was awake now. And probably wondering why the hell he was fondling her leg. He expected her to shy away from his touch, but she didn't. Instead, she sat up. She looked deep into his eyes for a moment, the fire of her passionate dream still lighting her gaze.

She reached up, cradling his face in her hands and tugging his mouth down to hers. He wasn't about to deny her. The moment their lips met, he felt the familiar surge of need wash over him. Before when they'd kissed, he had resisted the pull, but he couldn't do it any longer. He wanted her and she wanted him. They could deal with the consequences of it later.

Her mouth was hungry, demanding more of him, and he gave it. His tongue thrust inside her, matching her intensity and eliciting a groan deep in her throat. Her fingers drifted into his hair, desperately tugging him closer.

Gavin wrapped his arms around her waist and drew her up onto her knees. He explored every new curve of her body just as he'd fantasized, dipping low to cup the roundness of her backside. The firm press of her flesh against his fingertips was better than he ever could have imagined. He didn't think it was possible, but he grew even harder as he touched her.

Sabine's hands roamed as well, sliding down his chest, studying the ridges of his abs and then reaching around his back. She grasped the hem of his shirt and tugged until their lips parted and it came up and over his head. She did the same with her own shirt, throwing it to the floor and revealing full breasts with no bra to obscure them.

Before he could reach out to touch them, Sabine leaned back, cupping his neck with one hand and pulling him with her until she was lying on the couch and he was covering her body with his. Every soft inch of her molded to him. Her breasts crushed against his bare chest, the hard peaks of her nipples pressing insistently into his skin.

Gavin kissed her again and then let his lips roam along her jaw and down her throat. He teased at her sensitive skin, nipping gently with his teeth and soothing it with his tongue. He brought one palm to her breast, teasing the aching tip with slow circles and then massaging it with firm fingers. Sabine gasped aloud, her hips rising to meet his.

"I want you so badly," Gavin whispered against her collarbone.

Sabine didn't reply, but her hand eased between their bodies to unzip his jeans. She brought one finger up to her lips to gesture for him to be quiet, then her hand slipped under the waistband of his briefs. He fought for silence as her fingers wrapped around the length of him and stroked gently. He buried a moan against her breast, trying not to lose his grip of control. She knew just how to push him, just how to touch him to make him unravel.

He brushed her hand away and eased between her legs. He thrust his hips forward, creating a delicious friction as he rubbed against her through the thin cotton of her shorts.

"Ohh…" she whispered, her eyes closing.

She was so beautiful. He couldn't wait to watch her come undone. To bury himself deep inside her again after all this time.

"Please," he groaned, "tell me that you have something we can use." Gavin got up this morning thinking he was taking his son to the circus. He wasn't a teenager walking around with a condom in his pocket all the time. He hadn't come prepared for this.

Her eyes fluttered open, their green depths dark with desire. "I had an IUD put in after Jared was born," she said.

"Is that enough?" he asked.

At that, Sabine laughed. "It's supposed to be 99.8 percent effective, but with your super sperm, who knows? The condom didn't work so well for us the last time."

"Super sperm," Gavin snorted before dipping down

and kissing her again. "Do you want me to stop?" he asked. He would if she wanted him to, as much as that would kill him. But she needed to decide now.

"Don't you dare," she said, piercing him with her gaze.

With a growl, he buried his face in her neck. His hand grasped at the waist of her shorts, tugging them and her panties down over her hips. She arched up to help him and then kicked them off to the floor.

Sabine pushed at his jeans without success until Gavin finally eased back to take them off. She watched him with careful study as he kicked off his shoes and slipped out of the last of his clothes.

He looked down at her, nude and wanting, and his chest swelled with pride. She was sexy and free and waiting for him. As he watched, she reached up and untied her hair. The long strands fell down over her shoulders, the ends teasing at the tips of her breasts.

He couldn't wait any longer. Gavin returned to the couch, easing between her thighs. He sought her out first with his hand. Stroking gently, his fingertips slid easily over her sensitive flesh, causing her to whimper with need.

"Gavin," she pleaded, her voice little more than a breath.

His hand continued to move over her until she was panting and squirming beneath him. Then he slipped one finger inside. Sabine threw her head back, a cry strangling to silence in her throat. She was ready for him.

Gavin propped onto one elbow and gripped her hip with his other hand. Surging forward, he pressed into the slick heat of her welcoming body. He lost himself in the pleasure for a moment, absorbing every delicious sensation before flexing his hips and driving into her again.

Sabine clung to him, burying her face in his shoulder to muffle her gasps and cries. She met his every advance, whispering words of encouragement into his ear. The intensity built, moment by moment, until he knew she was close.

Her eyes squeezed shut, her mouth falling open in silent gasps. He put every ounce of energy he had left into pushing her over the edge. He was rewarded with the soft shudder of her body against him, the muscles deep inside clenching around him. The string of tension in his belly drew tighter and tighter until it snapped. He thrust hard, exploding into her with a low growl of satisfaction.

They both collapsed against the couch cushions in a panting, gasping heap. No sooner had they recovered than Gavin heard Jared crying in the other room.

Sabine pressed against his chest until he backed off. She quickly tugged on her clothes and disappeared into the bedroom.

Things were officially more complicated.

Six

Jared went back down fairly quickly. Sabine changed his Pull-Ups, put him in his pajamas and he fell asleep in minutes. Even then, she stayed in her bedroom longer than necessary. Going back into the living room meant facing what she'd just done. She wasn't quite ready for that yet.

Damn that stupid, erotic dream. When she fell asleep on the couch, she never expected to sleep that long. Or that she would have a sexual fantasy about Gavin while he was sitting there watching her. When she opened her eyes and he was touching her with the spark of passion in his eyes, she had to have him. She needed him.

And now it was done. She'd refused his proposal of marriage because he didn't love her, yet she'd just slept with him. She was throwing mixed signals left, right and center.

But she had to go back out there eventually. Steeling

her resolve, she exited the bedroom and pulled the door shut behind her. She made a quick stop in the restroom first, cleaning up and smoothing her hair back into a ponytail. When she returned to the living room, Gavin was fully dressed and sitting on the couch.

"Everything okay?" he asked.

"Yeah," she said. "He's back to sleep now. He probably won't wake up again until the morning." She nervously ran her hands over her shorts, not sure what to do with herself. "Did you guys have fun today?"

"We did. He's a very well-behaved kid. Gave me almost no trouble. Almost," he said with a smile.

Sabine was glad. She'd worried so much about them that she couldn't paint. At least at first. She'd tried, but it had been so long since she'd painted that she didn't know where to start. Instead, she'd taken a long, leisurely shower and indulged in extended grooming rituals she usually had to rush, like plucking her eyebrows and painting her toenails. One of her favorite chick flicks was on TV, so she sat down to watch it, and the next thing she knew, she was nodding off. She'd only expected to sleep for a half hour or so.

"I'm glad it went well." She eyed the spot on the couch where she'd just been and decided she wasn't quite ready to sit there yet. "Would you like some wine? I'm going to pour myself a glass."

"Sure," he said with a soft smile.

Sabine could tell this was awkward for him, too. And yet, he could've turned her down and left. But he didn't. She disappeared into the kitchen and returned a few minutes later with two glasses of merlot. "It came out of a box, but I like it," she said.

Gavin smiled in earnest, taking a large sip, then another. "It's pretty good," he admitted with surprise.

She sat down beside him and took her own sip. The wine seemed to flow directly into her veins, relaxing her immediately.

He pointed over at the blank canvas. "I'm surprised you didn't paint at all today."

Sabine looked at the white expanse that had been her nemesis for a good part of the afternoon. She couldn't count how many times she'd put her pencil to the canvas to sketch the bones of a scene and then stopped. "I think I've forgotten how to paint."

"That's not possible," Gavin argued. "You just need the right inspiration. I put you on the spot today. I bet if you relax and let the creative juices flow without the pressure of time, the ideas will come again."

"I hope so."

"You're too gifted to set your dream aside. Even for Jared. We can work together to get you back to what you love. I mean, after we get the results and I have visitation rights, you'll have more free time to yourself."

That was the wrong thing to say. She had been nervous enough about tomorrow and the lab results that were coming in. Knowing he was already planning to "exercise his rights" and take Jared for long stretches of time just made her chest tight with anxiety. It was a sharp reminder that even after they'd had sex, he was really here for Jared, not her. He hadn't mentioned anything about *all* of them spending time together. Or just the two of them. Any fantasies she had about there being any sort of family unit cobbled out of this mess were just that.

"And what about you?" she said, her tone a bit sharper than she'd planned. "You seem as wrapped up in the business as ever. We couldn't get you off your phone yesterday. I'm thinking you don't have much time to get in the cockpit anymore."

"It's been a while," he admitted. "But I'm working on it. All those calls I was taking at the zoo," he said, "were about a big deal I'm trying to pull together. Things were unraveling and I couldn't let it happen."

Sabine listened as he described his plans for BXS and Exclusivity Jetliners. It really did seem like a brilliant plan. There were plenty of wealthy and important people who would pay a premium for that kind of service. That didn't mean she appreciated it interloping on their day out together, but she could see it was important to him and not just day-to-day management crap.

"I'm hoping to fly one, too."

Her brows went up in surprise. "Did you get demoted from CEO to pilot?"

"I wish," he groaned. "But I've always wanted a Gulf-stream model jet. The ones we're acquiring could go over four thousand miles on one tank of gas. That could get me to Paris. I've always dreamed of flying across the Atlantic. But even if I can't manage that, I can take one out from time to time. Even if it's just to do a delivery. I don't care. I just want to get out from behind the desk and get up there. It's the only place I can ever find any peace."

She understood that. Yoga did a lot to help center her mind and spirit, but nothing came close to losing herself in her art.

"I want more time out of the office, and Jared finally gives me a real reason to do it. There's no point in work-life balance when you've got no life. But spending time with Jared needs to be a priority for me. I've already missed so much."

Sabine was impressed by his heartfelt words. Gavin had quickly become enamored with Jared, and she was glad. Part of her had always worried that he might reject his son. The other part worried that he'd claim him with such force that he'd rip her child from her arms. This seemed a healthy medium. Maybe this wouldn't be so bad. He was trying.

"I found a great apartment in Greenwich Village overlooking Washington Square Park," he said. "It has three bedrooms and it's close to the subway."

Sabine took a large sip of her wine. Here we go, she thought. "I thought you liked your apartment," she said, playing dumb. "Getting tired of living at the Ritz-Carlton?"

Gavin frowned. "What? No. Not for me. For you. I'd prefer you to be closer to me, but I know you'd rather live downtown. You work in SoHo, right? You could easily walk to work from this apartment."

Walking to work. She wouldn't even allow herself to fantasize about a life without a long train commute each day. Or three bedrooms where she didn't have to share with Jared. "I'm pretty sure it's out of my budget."

Gavin set his wine down on the coffee table. "I told you I wanted to help. Let me buy you an apartment."

"And I told you I wanted to take this slowly. I probably couldn't even afford the maintenance fee, much less the taxes or the mortgage itself. Homeowner's insurance. The utilities on a place that large would be through the roof."

He turned in his seat to face her, his serious businessman expression studying her. "How much is your rent here?"

"Gavin, I—"

He interrupted her with a number that was fewer than fifty dollars off the mark.

"Yes, pretty much," she admitted, reluctantly.

"Tack on a couple hundred for utilities and such. So what if I bought an apartment and rented it to you for the same amount you're paying now? That would be fair, right? You wouldn't have to worry about all the fees associated with owning the place."

She did have to admit that she preferred this idea. If she had to pay rent, she would continue working. She liked her job and wanted to keep doing it. But a three-bedroom apartment in the Village for the price of what she paid for a tiny place beyond the reach of the subway lines? That was insanity.

"That's a ridiculous suggestion. My rent is less than a tenth of what the mortgage on that kind of apartment would be."

Gavin shrugged. "I'm not concerned. You could live there rent-free for all I care. I just thought you would feel more comfortable if you contributed."

"There's a difference between helping us out and buying us a multimillion-dollar apartment."

"I want you close," he said. His dark eyes penetrated hers with an intensity that made her squirm slightly with a flush rising to her pale cheeks. Did he really mean *her?*

Sabine opened her mouth to argue, but he held up his hand to silence her protest. "I mean," he corrected, "living in Manhattan will make it easier to handle the custody arrangements and trade-offs. When he starts at his new school, he would be closer. It would be safer. More convenient for everyone."

Just as she thought. He wanted Jared close, not her. At least not for any reason more than the occasional booty call. "Especially for you," she snapped, irritably.

"And you!" he added. "If I got things my way, the two of you would just move in with me. That's certainly the cheapest option, since you seem so concerned about how much I spend, but I thought you would like having your own space better."

She must seem like the most ungrateful person on the planet, but she knew what this was. A slippery slope. He would push, push, push until he had things just the way he wanted them. If he wanted them—or Jared, she should say—living with him, eventually he would. This apartment in the Village would just be a pit stop to make it look as if he was being reasonable.

"I know it's a pain for you to drive all the way out here every time you want to see Jared. And I know that you and I just…" Her voice trailed off.

"Had sex?" he offered.

"Yes," she said with a heavy sigh. "But that doesn't change anything between us or about the things we've already discussed. We're not moving at all. Not in with you and not into that apartment. It sounds nice, but it's too soon. When we're ready, perhaps we could look together. I'd like some say in the decision, even if you're writing the checks. I'm pretty sure the place I pick will be significantly cheaper."

"I'm not concerned with the cost of keeping my child happy and safe."

A painful twinge nagged at Sabine right beneath her sternum. She should be happy the father of her child was willing to lay out millions for the health and welfare of their child. But a part of her was jealous. He was always so quick to point out that this was about their son. Each time he mentioned it, it was like he was poking the gaping wound of her heart with a sharp stick. She would benefit from the arrangement, but none of this was about her. The sex didn't change anything, just like it didn't change anything three years ago. He was attracted to her, but she was not his priority and never was.

"Thank you," she choked out. "I appreciate that you're so willing to create a stable, safe home for our son. Let's give it a week to sink in, all right? We've got a lot of hurdles to jump before we add real estate to the mix."

Gavin eyed her for a moment before silently nodding. Sabine knew this was anything but a victory. She was only pushing off the inevitable. He would get his way eventually.

He always did.

When Gavin arrived at Dr. Peterson's office at 10:00 a.m. Monday morning, Sabine was already there. She was lost in a fashion magazine and didn't notice him come in. "Morning," he said.

Sabine looked up and gave him a watery smile. "Hey." She looked a little out of sorts. Maybe she was nervous. Things would change after this and she probably knew it.

"Where's Jared?" he asked.

The smile faded. She slung the magazine she'd been reading onto the seat beside her. "At school, where he belongs. I'm sorry to disappoint, but you're stuck with me today."

He'd screwed up last night, he could tell. Not in seducing her—that would never be a bad idea—but in forcing the idea of the apartment on her. Anyone else would jump at the offer, but to her, it was him imposing on her. Demanding they be closer so he could see his son more easily. Not once mentioning that he'd like *her* closer as well because that opened the door to dangerous territory.

Sabine was skittish. She scared off easily last time. He wasn't about to tell her that he wanted to see her more because he was still fighting himself over the idea of it. He was usually pretty good at keeping his distance from people, but he'd already let Sabine in once. Keeping her out the second time was harder than he expected. Especially when he didn't want to. He wanted her in his bed. Across from him at a nice restaurant. Certainly he could have that and not completely lose himself to her.

"That's scarcely a hardship," he said, seating himself in the empty chair beside her. "I find your company to be incredibly…*stimulating.*"

Sabine crossed her arms over her chest and smothered a snort of disbelief. "Well, you'll be stimulating yourself from now on. Last night was—"

"Awesome?" he interjected. Their physical connection could never be anything less.

"A mistake."

"Sometimes a mistake can be a happy accident. Like Jared, a happy accident."

Her moss-green eyes narrowed at him. "And sometimes it's just a mistake. Like sleeping with your ex when you're in the middle of a custody negotiation."

Gavin nodded and leaned into her, crossing his own arms. She really thought last night was a mistake? He hadn't picked up on it at the time. She was probably just worried it would give him the upper hand somehow. Knowing just how to touch a woman was always an advantage, but he didn't intend to use that knowledge against her. At least outside the bedroom.

"So I suppose you've got no business going to dinner with me tonight, either."

Her gaze ran over his face, trying to read into his motives. "Listen, Gavin," she started with a shake of her head. "I know I told you that I wanted you to put in quality time with Jared, but that doesn't mean you have to come see him *every* day. I know you've got a company to run and a life in progress before all this came out. I only meant that you had to keep your promises and make an effort."

She thought this was about Jared. Apparently he had not made it abundantly clear how badly he wanted her last night. Their tryst on the couch was nice, but it was just an appetizer to take the edge off three years apart. He wouldn't allow himself to fall for Sabine, but he wasn't going to deny himself the pleasure of making love to her. "Who said anything about Jared? I was thinking about you and me. Someplace dark and quiet with no kid's menu."

"That sounds lovely," she said, "but Jared isn't a puppy. We can't just crate him while we go out."

"I can arrange for someone to watch him."

A flicker of conflict danced across her face. She wanted to go. He could tell. She was just very protective and worried about leaving their son with a stranger. Hell, she hadn't even wanted to leave Jared with *him*.

"Someone? You don't even know who?"

"Of course I do. I was actually considering my secretary, Marie. She's got a new grandson of her own that she fawns over, but he lives in Vermont, so she doesn't see him nearly as much as she wants to. I asked her this morning if she was willing to watch Jared tonight. She'll even come out to your apartment so you don't have to pack up any of his things and he can sleep in his own bed when the time comes."

Sabine pursed her lips in thought and flipped her ponytail over her shoulder. "So you were so confident that I would go to dinner with you that you arranged a babysitter before you even bothered to ask if I wanted to go."

Her dream last night had tipped her hand. "Your subconscious doesn't lie."

Her cheeks flushed red against her pale complexion. She turned away from him and focused her attention on the television mounted on the opposite wall of the waiting room. "What if I have plans?"

"Do you have plans?" he asked.

"No," she admitted without facing him. "But that's not the point. You assume too much. You assume that just because we have a child together and we went too far last night that I want—"

"Brooks!" The nurse opened the side door and called out their name to come back.

Sabine's concerned expression faded, the lines disappearing between her brows. She seemed relieved to avoid this conversation. He wasn't going to let her off that easily.

"To be continued," Gavin said, looking her square in the eye. She met his gaze and nodded softly.

He climbed to his feet and offered his hand to help Sabine up. They made their way back to Dr. Peterson's personal office and sat in the two guest chairs across from his desk. It didn't take long before his physician strolled in with a file in his hands.

Dr. Peterson eased into his seat and flipped open the

paperwork. His gaze ran over it for a moment before he nodded. In that brief flash of time, Gavin had his first flicker of doubt. Jared looked just like him. There was no real reason to believe he wasn't his son, but Sabine had seemed nervous in the lobby. He didn't know anything for certain until the doctor told him the results. He hadn't even wanted a son a week ago, and now he would be devastated to know Jared wasn't his.

"Well," the doctor began, "I've got good news for you, Mr. Brooks. It appears as though you're a father. Congratulations," he said, reaching across the desk to shake his hand.

"Thank you," Gavin replied with relief washing over him.

Dr. Peterson pulled out two manila envelopes and handed one to each of them. "Here's a copy of the DNA report for each of you to give your lawyers."

This apparently was not the doctor's first paternity test rodeo. "Thank you," he said, slipping the envelope into his lapel pocket.

"Let me know if you have any questions. Good luck to you both." Dr. Peterson stood, ushering them out the door.

They were back in the lobby of the building before they spoke again. Gavin turned to her as she was putting the envelope into her purse. "Now about that dinner. You never answered me."

Sabine looked up at him. She didn't have the relieved expression he was expecting. She seemed even more concerned than she had going in. "Not tonight, Gavin. I'm not much in the mood for that."

"What's the matter?" he asked. Some women would be leaping with joy to have scientific evidence that their child was the heir to a multibillion-dollar empire. Sabine was a notable exception. "This was your idea," he reminded her.

She sighed. "I know. And I knew what the results would be, but I wasn't prepared for the finality of it. It's done. Now the wheels start turning and the child that has been one hundred percent mine for the past two years will start slipping from my arms. It's selfish of me, I know, and I apologize, but that doesn't make me leap for joy."

Gavin turned to face her, placing his hands reassuringly on her shoulders. It gave her no real choice but to look at him. "Sabine, what can I possibly say to convince you that this isn't a bad thing?"

Her pale green eyes grew glassy with tears she was too stubborn to shed in front of him. "There's nothing you can say, Gavin. Actions speak louder than words."

Fair enough. "How about this," he offered. "I'll get Edmund to start the paperwork and put together a custody proposal for you to look over. When you're happy with it, we'll share a nice dinner, just the two of us, to celebrate that the sky didn't fall and things will be fine."

Her gaze dropped to his collar and she nodded so slightly, he could barely tell she'd agreed. "Okay," she whispered.

"Clear your schedule for Friday night," he said with confidence. "I have a feeling we're going to be sharing a lovely candlelit dinner together before the weekend arrives."

Sabine curled up on the couch and watched Gavin and Jared play on the living room floor. They were stacking Duplo blocks. Gavin was trying to build a plane, but

Jared was determined to make a truck and kept stealing pieces off the clunky blue-and-red jet. It was amazing to see them together, the father and his tiny toddler clone.

It made her smile, even when she wasn't sure she should be smiling.

Gavin had done his best to reassure her that things would be fine. His lawyer had presented a very reasonable custody agreement. Her relief at reading the briefing was palpable. They were both giving a little and taking a little, which surprised her. Gavin got Jared on alternate weekends, rotating holidays and two weeks in the summer, but he would continue to reside primarily with Sabine. Her concession was to agree to move to Manhattan to make the arrangement easier on everyone.

They'd built in flexibility in the agreement to accommodate special requests, like birthdays. Unless Gavin pushed her, she intended to let him see Jared as often as he liked. How could she turn away a scene like the one playing out on her floor?

Tonight, they were telling Jared that Gavin was his father. It was a big moment for them. The DNA test had made it certain, but telling Jared made it real.

"Hey, big guy?" Gavin said.

Jared dropped a block and looked up. "Yep?"

"Do you know what a daddy is?"

Sabine leaned forward in her seat, resting her elbows on her knees. She agreed to let Gavin be the one to tell him, but she wasn't certain how much Jared would understand. He was still so young.

"Yeah," he said cheerfully, before launching into another of his long-winded and unintelligible speeches. Jared was a quiet child, slow to speak, although it seemed more that he didn't have a lot he wanted to say.

Only in the past few months had he started rattling on in his own toddler-speak. From what pieces she could pick out, he was talking about his friend at school whose daddy picked him up every day. Then he pointed at Sabine. "Mommy."

"Right." Gavin smiled. "And I am *your* daddy."

Jared cocked his head to the side and wrinkled his nose. He turned to Sabine for confirmation. "Daddy?"

She let out the breath she'd been holding to nod. "Yeah, buddy. He's your daddy."

A peculiar grin crossed Jared's face. It was the same expression he made when she "stole" his nose and he wasn't quite sure he believed her. "Daddy?" He pointed at Gavin.

Gavin nodded, having only a moment to brace himself before his son launched into his arms.

"Daddy!" he proclaimed.

Sabine watched Gavin hold his son as fiercely as if someone were going to snatch him away. She understood how he felt. And then she saw the glassy tears in the eyes of her powerful CEO, and her chest tightened with the rush of confusing emotions. It hadn't taken long, but Gavin was completely in love with his son.

She couldn't help but feel a pang of jealousy.

Seven

"Damn you for always being right."

Gavin stood on Sabine's doorstep holding a bouquet of purple dahlias. She had opened the door and greeted him that way, stealing his "hello" from his lips. Fortunately she was smiling, so he did the same.

He held out the bundle of flowers with the nearly black centers that faded to bright purple tips. "These are for you. They reminded me of your hair."

Sabine brought the flowers up to her nose and delicately inhaled their scent. "They're beautiful, thank you."

"So are you," he added. And he meant it. She looked lovely tonight. She was wearing a fitted white dress with brightly colored flowers that looked like one of her watercolor paintings. It was sleeveless and clung to every curve of her body.

She smiled, wrinkling her nose with a touch of embarrassment. The movement caught the light on the tiny pink rhinestone in her nose. It was the same bright color as her lipstick and the chunky bracelet on her wrist. "Let me put these in some water and we can go."

Gavin nodded and stepped across the threshold into the apartment. It was Friday night and as predicted, they were having dinner. Everything had gone smoothly. The paperwork had been filed in family court to add Gavin's name to the birth certificate. Along with the addition, Jared's last name would be updated to Brooks. He'd suggested making Jared's middle name Hayes, but she said the name Thomas was more important to her. He'd thought Sabine would pitch a fit on the subject of Jared's name, but it hadn't concerned her.

The custody proposal Edmund put together was approved by both of them on the first draft. He hoped that he would see Jared more than required, but this established a minimum they were both comfortable with.

He noticed Marie's coat hanging by the door when he came in, so he knew she was already there to watch Jared. Gavin looked around the apartment, but he didn't see Marie or Jared anywhere. "Where is everyone?"

Then he heard giggles and splashing from the bathroom. He smiled, knowing Marie was probably soaked. After they'd told Jared that Gavin was his daddy, he'd insisted *Daddy* give him his bath that night. Gavin had gotten more water on him than the toddler in the tub, he was pretty certain.

Aside from that, the night had gone pretty smoothly. Apparently toddlers didn't angst about things the way grown-ups did. Gavin was his daddy—*great.* Let's go play.

"Marie is giving Jared a bath, although I think they're

probably having more fun with the bathtub paints than actually washing."

Gavin wanted to peek in and say hello before they left, but he resisted. He'd gotten Sabine to agree to this dinner and the babysitter he provided. Right now, Jared was happy. If they went in to say goodbye, the giggles might disintegrate into tears. "Are you ready?"

She nodded, the luxurious black waves of her hair gracefully swaying along her jawline. "I already told Marie goodbye a few minutes ago so we could slip out. She seems to have everything under control."

Since it was just the two of them tonight, he'd opted for the Aston Martin. He held the door for her, noting the elegant curve of her ankles in tall pink pumps as she slipped inside. Gavin had no clue how women walked in shoes like that, but he was extremely thankful they did.

They had seven-thirty reservations at one of the most sought-out, high-end restaurants in Manhattan. He'd made the reservation on Monday, feeling confident they would come to an agreement in time, but even then, it had taken some persuading to get a table. Most people booked a table several months in advance, but they knew better than to tell a Brooks no. He tended to get in wherever he wanted to, and he made it worth the maître d's efforts.

They checked in and were immediately taken to an intimate booth for two. The restaurant was the brain-child of a young, up-and-coming chef who snagged a James Beard award at the unheard-of age of twenty-two. The decor was decidedly modern with lots of glass, concrete and colored lights that glowed behind geometric wall panels.

Their table was like a cocoon wrapping around them

and shielding them from the world. A green glass container on the table had a flickering candle inside, giving a moody light to their space. It was just enough to read their menus, but not enough to draw attention to who was inside the booth. It made the restaurant popular with the young celebrity set who wanted to go out but maintain their privacy.

"Have you ever been here?" Gavin asked.

Sabine took in all the sights with wide eyes. "No, but I've heard of it. My boss said her husband took her here for her birthday."

"Did she like it?"

"She said the food was good. The decor was a little modern for her taste, which is funny considering her clothing design has a contemporary edge to it that would fit right in."

"I've been here once," Gavin said. "It's fine cuisine, but it's not stuffy. I thought you'd like that."

Sabine smiled and looked down. "Yes, there aren't fifteen pieces of silverware, so that's a relief."

Gavin smiled and looked over the menu. He'd learned his lesson the first time they dated. His attempts to impress her with nice restaurants had only intimidated her and pointed out the wide gap of their social standings. She wasn't like other women he'd dated. A lot of women in Manhattan expected to be wined and dined in the finest restaurants in town. Sabine was just as happy with Thai takeout eaten on the terrace of his apartment, if not more so.

This place was his attempt at a compromise and so far, it seemed to be a good choice. There wasn't a fixed tasting menu like so many other restaurants. Foie gras and caviar wasn't her style, and she wouldn't let him pay two hundred dollars a head for a meal she wouldn't eat.

Here, diners got to mix and match their choice of Asian fusion dishes for the six courses.

The waiter brought their drinks, presenting him with a premium sake and Sabine with a light green pear martini that was nearly the color of her eyes. They ordered and the server disappeared to bring their first course selection.

"I'm glad we got everything worked out with Edmund. I've been looking forward to this night all week." He met her eyes across the table and let a knowing smile curl his lips. Gavin expected tonight to go well and for Sabine to end up back in his bed. He'd fantasized about her naked body lying across his sheets as he lay in bed each night.

Holding up his drink for a toast, he waited for Sabine to do the same. "To surviving the terrible twos," he said with a grin, "and everything else the future may hold."

Sabine tipped her glass against his and took a healthy sip. "Thank you for handling all of this so gingerly. You don't know how much I've worried."

"What are we drinking to?" A nasal voice cut into their conversation.

They both turned to find a blonde woman standing beside their table. *Ugh.* It was Viola Collins. The Manhattan society busybody was one of the last people he wanted to see tonight. She had a big mouth, an overabundance of opinions and a blatant desire for Gavin that he'd dodged for years.

"Viola," he said, ignoring her question and wishing he could ignore her, as well. "How are you?"

She smiled and showed off her perfect set of straightened, whitened teeth that looked a touch odd against her too-tan skin. "I'm just great." Her laser focus shifted toward Sabine, taking in and categorizing every detail with visible distaste. "And who do we have here?"

Gavin watched his date with concern. He wasn't certain how Sabine would react to someone like Viola. Some people might shrink away under Viola's obvious appraisal, but she didn't. Sabine sat up straighter in her seat and met Viola's gaze with her own confident one.

"Viola Collins, this is my date, Sabine Hayes."

The women briefly shook hands, but he could tell there was no friendliness behind it. Women were funny that way, sizing one another up under the cool guise of politeness.

"Would I have met you before?" Viola asked.

"I sincerely doubt it," Sabine replied.

Gavin couldn't remember if they had or not. "You may have. Sabine and I dated a few years back."

"Hmm…" Viola said. Her nose turned up slightly, although Gavin thought that might be more the result of her latest round of plastic surgery. "I think I would've remembered *this*. That's interesting that you two are dating again. I would've thought the novelty would've worn off the first time."

"Oh, no," Sabine said, a sharp edge to her voice. "I'm very bendy."

Viola's eyes widened, her tight mouth twisting at Sabine's bold words. "Are you?" She turned to Gavin. "Well, I'll have to tell Rosemary Goodwin that you're off the market. *For now*," she added. "I think she's still waiting for you to call her again after your last hot date. I'll just tell her to be patient."

"You'll have to excuse me." Sabine reached for her purse and slipped out of the booth, deliberately sweeping the green martini off the table. The concoction splattered across Viola's cream silk dress. "How clumsy of me!"

she said. Ignoring the sputtering woman, Sabine bent down to pick up the glass and set it back on the table. "That's better." At that, she turned and bolted from the restaurant.

Viola gawked at Sabine as she disappeared, sputtering in outrage. The silk dress was ruined. No question of it.

Gavin didn't care. Viola could use a fist to the face, but no one wanted to pick up her plastic surgery tab to repair the damage. He got up, throwing cash onto the table for the bill and pressing more into Viola's hand for a new dress. "That wasn't your color anyway."

He jogged through the restaurant, pushing through the crowd waiting to be seated, and bursting out onto the street. He spied Sabine about a block away, charging furiously down the pavement despite the handicap of her heels.

"Sabine!" he yelled. "Wait."

She didn't even turn around. He had to run to catch up with her, pulling alongside and matching her stride.

"I should've known," she said, without acknowledging him. "You know there was a reason I ended this the last time. One of the reasons was that everyone in your world is a snob."

"Not everyone," he insisted. He wrapped his fingers around her delicate wrist to keep her from running off again and pulled her to a stop. "Just ignore Viola. She doesn't matter to anyone but herself."

She shook her head, the waves of her hair falling into her face as she looked down at the sidewalk. "It's the same as last time, Gavin. People in your world are never going to see me as anything other than an interloper. Like you're slumming for your own amusement. I don't fit in and I never will."

"I know," he said. "That's one of the many things that make you great."

Her light green eyes met his for a moment, a glimmer of something—hope, maybe—quickly fading away. "Stop fooling yourself, Gavin. You belong with someone like Viola or this Rosemary woman that's waiting on you to call again. We're all wrong for each other. You're only here with me now because of Jared."

"Let me assure you that if I wanted a woman like Viola I could have one. I could have *her,* if I wanted to. She's made that very clear over the years, but I'm not interested. I don't want her." He took a step closer, pulling Sabine against him. "I want you. Just as you are."

"You say that now, but you wouldn't answer her question," she said, resisting his pull on her.

"Answer what question?"

"She asked what we were drinking to. You don't want anyone to know about Jared, do you? Are you ashamed of him? Or of both of us?"

"Absolutely not!" he said as emphatically as he could. "I will gladly shout the news about my son from the rooftops. But I haven't told my family yet. If Viola found out, it would be all over town. I don't want them to hear it from her."

Gavin slipped his arms around her waist, enjoying the feel of her against him, even under these circumstances. "I'd like to tell them tomorrow afternoon. Would you be able to bring Jared to meet them? Maybe around dinnertime? That would give them some time to adjust to the idea before you show up."

"Why don't you just come get him?" she said. Her bravado from her interaction with Viola had crumbled. Now she just looked worn down.

"Because I want them to spend time with you, too,"

Gavin added. "I know you've met them before, but that was years ago. This is different."

"And say what, Gavin? 'Hey, everyone, you remember Sabine? Since you saw her last, she's had my son and lied to all of us for over two years. We've got that worked out now. Don't mind the nose ring.'"

"Pretty much," he said with a smile. "How did you guess?"

Sabine's gaze shot up to his. Red flushed her cheeks and she punched him in the shoulder. She hit him as furiously as she could and he barely felt it. He laughed at her assault, which only made it worse. She was like an angry kitten, hissing and clawing, but not dangerous enough to even break the skin. "I'm serious, Gavin!"

"I'm serious, too." He meant every word of it. Gavin had gone into this thinking that he could indulge in Sabine's body and keep his heart thoroughly out of the equation. She had no idea how badly she'd hurt him when she left, and he didn't want her to know. But he'd opened the door to her once. No matter how hard he fought, it was too easy to open up to her again. It wasn't love, but it was something more than his usual indifference.

Perhaps this time would be different. Even if they weren't together, they would always be connected through Jared. They would be constants in an ever-changing life and he welcomed it, even if he didn't know what they would do with it.

He slipped his finger under her chin and tipped her face up to him. "Serious about this."

Gavin's lips met hers before she could start arguing with him again. The moment he kissed her, she was lost. She melted into him, channeling her emotions into the kiss. Sabine let all of her anger, her frustration, her fear flow through her mouth and her fingertips. She buried her fingers through his dark hair, tugging his neck closer.

He responded in kind, his mouth punishing her with his kiss. His hands molded to her body, his fingers pressed hard into her flesh. The rough touch was a pleasure with a razor's edge. She craved his intensity. The physical connection made everything else fade away. At least for tonight. Tomorrow was…tomorrow.

"Take me to your place," she said.

Gavin reluctantly pulled away. "I'll have the valet bring the car."

Within a few minutes, they were strolling into the Ritz-Carlton Tower. They took the elevator up to Gavin's apartment. It had been a long time since she'd been here. She'd walked alone down this very hallway after she broke up with him. Pregnant and unaware of that fact. It felt strange to traverse the same carpeting after all these years.

Inside the apartment, little had changed. The same elegant, expensive and uncomfortable furniture that was better suited for a decorating magazine than to actually being used. The same stunning view of Central Park sprawled out of the arched floor-to-ceiling windows. There was a newer, larger, flatter television mounted to one wall, but that was about it.

"You've done a lot with the place since I saw it last," she said drily.

"There's new additions," he insisted. He pointed to a corner in the dining room where there was a stack of children's toys, new in the packages, and the car seat from the Mercedes. "I'm also doing some renovations to one of the bedrooms."

Gavin led her down the hallway to the rooms that had once functioned as a guest room and his office. Inside the old guest room, a tarp was draped over the hardwood floors. Several cans of paint were sitting in the middle of the floor, unopened. Construction was under way for some wainscoting and a window seat that would cover and vent the radiators. Jared was too young to enjoy it now, but she could just imagine him curling up there, looking out over Central Park and reading a book.

"You said his favorite color was red, so I was going to paint the walls red." He gestured over to the side. "I'm having them build a loft with a ladder into this niche here, so he'll have his own tree house–like space to play when he's older. They're delivering a toddler bed in a few days with a Spider-Man bedding set and curtains."

"It's wonderful," Sabine said. And it was. A million times better than anything she could afford to get him. "He will love it, especially when he gets a little older. What little boy wouldn't?"

Sabine took a last look and moved back out into the hallway and past the closed door to his home office. She didn't begrudge her son anything his father gave him, but it was hard for her to face that Gavin could provide Jared with things she couldn't. "What's this?" she asked, pointing toward a touch panel on the table near the phone.

Gavin caught up with her in the living room. "It's the new Ritz-Carlton concierge system. We didn't have dinner. Would you like me to order something?"

"Maybe later. It's still early." Sabine kicked off her heels and continued through the apartment to the master suite. She reached behind her and began unzipping her dress as she disappeared around the corner.

She'd barely made it three feet inside before she felt Gavin's heat against her back. He brushed her hands away, tugging her zipper down the curve of her spine. His fingertips brushed at the soft skin there, just briefly, before he moved to her shoulders and pushed her dress off.

Sabine stepped out of her clothing, continuing across the room in nothing but the white satin bra and panties she'd worn with it. There were no lights on in that room, so she was free to walk to the window and look outside without being seen.

She heard Gavin close the door behind them, ensuring they were blanketed in darkness. The moonlight from outside was enough to illuminate the pieces of furniture she remembered from before.

She felt Gavin's breath on her neck before he touched her. His bare chest pushed into her back, his skin hot and firm. He swept her hair over her left shoulder, leaning down to press searing kisses along the line of her neck. One bra strap was pushed aside, then the other, before he unhooked the clasp and let the satin fall to the floor.

Sabine relaxed against him, letting her head roll back to rest on his shoulder and expose her throat. She closed her eyes to block out the distraction of the view and focus on the feeling of his lips, teeth and tongue moving over her sensitive flesh. His palms covered her exposed breasts, molding them with his hands and gently pinching the tips until she whimpered aloud with pleasure.

"Sabine," he whispered, biting at her earlobe. "You don't know how long I've waited to have you back in my bed." He slid his hands down to her hips, holding her steady as he pressed his arousal into her backside with a growl.

The vibration of the sound rumbled through her whole body like a shock wave. Her nipples tightened and her core pulsed with need. Knowing she could turn him on like this was such a high. She never felt as sexy as she did when she was with Gavin. Somehow, knowing she could bring such a powerful man to his knees with desire and pleasure was the greatest turn-on.

Sabine turned in his arms, looking up at the dark shadows across his face before she smiled and slipped out of his grasp. Her eyes had adjusted to the light. It made it easy for her to find her way to the massive bed in the center of his room. She crawled up onto it, throwing a glance over her shoulder to make sure he was watching the swell of her backside peeking out from the satin panties. Of course he was.

"This bed?" she asked sweetly, although she felt anything but sweet.

Gavin had his hands balled into fists at his side. "What are you trying to do to me?"

He was fighting for control, but she didn't want him to win. She wanted him to break, to lose himself in her. It would only require her to push a little bit harder. She climbed up to her knees and hooked her thumbs beneath her panties. Looking him in the eye, she bit her lips and glided the slick fabric over her hips.

His breath was ragged in his chest, but he held his place. Gavin's burning gaze danced between the bite of her teeth into her plump pink lips to her full, pert breasts, to the ever-lowering panties. When the cropped dark curls of her sex peeked out from the top, he swallowed hard. His hands went to his belt. His eyes never left her body as he removed the last of his clothes.

Now they were both naked with no more barriers between them. She was ready for him to unleash his passion on her.

With a wicked smile, Sabine flicked her dark hair over her shoulder and curled her finger to beckon Gavin to come to her. He didn't hesitate, surging forward onto the bed until she fell backward onto the soft comforter.

Every inch of her was suddenly covered by the massive expanse of his body. The weight of him pressed her into the mattress, molding her against him. He entered her quickly as well, causing Sabine to cry out before she could stop herself.

"Yes," Gavin hissed in encouragement. "Be loud. You can scream the walls down tonight." He thrust hard into her again. "I want hotel security knocking on the door."

Sabine laughed and drew her knees up to cradle him. When he surged forward again, he drove deeper. She groaned loud, the sound echoing off the walls of the room. He wanted her loud and she would be happy to oblige.

Eight

Sabine rang the doorbell with her elbow, fighting to keep ahold of her son. Jared squirmed furiously in her arms, and she didn't blame him. For their trip to see Gavin's parents she'd dressed him in his best outfit— a pair of khakis, a short-sleeved plaid shirt and a little bow tie. Adrienne had bought the outfit for him and he looked adorable in it. When he stopped squirming. His two-year-old heart much preferred hoodies and T-shirts with cartoon characters on them.

Putting him on the ground, she crouched down to his level and straightened his clothes. "Hey, buddy," she said. "I know you don't like this, but I need you to be a good boy today. You're going to see Daddy and meet some nice people who are very excited to see you."

"Don't wanna." He pouted, with one lip sticking out so far, she was tempted to kiss it away. "Want truck."

"I've got your truck in my bag, and you can have it later. If you're a good boy today, we'll get ice cream on the way home, okay?"

The dark, mischievous eyes of her son looked up at her, considering the offer. Before he could answer, the door opened and Sabine looked up into the same eyes. Gavin was in the doorway.

"Hi, Jared," Gavin said, his whole face lighting up at the sight of his son. He knelt down and put out his arms, and Jared immediately stopped pouting and ran to him. Gavin scooped him up and swung him in the air while Jared giggled hysterically.

Sabine stood and smiled, nervously readjusting her purse on her shoulder and smoothing a hand over her hair. She'd pulled the black-and-purple strands back into a bun at the nape of her neck. The violet highlights were still visible, but not so "in their face." Adrienne had insisted she wear one of her newly designed tops today, a silky, scoop-neck red top that gathered at the waist. She'd paired it with some black pants and a patent leather belt. It looked good on her, but it was hardly the armor she'd wanted going into this.

She sucked a deep breath into her lungs, trying to even out her frantic heartbeat, but it did little good. She was about to see Gavin's parents again, and this time, as the mother of their grandchild. They had been polite but distant the last time. Obviously, they hadn't felt the need to get invested in Gavin's latest dating novelty.

She didn't anticipate this going well. They might hate her for keeping Jared a secret. They might turn their noses up at her like Viola had. Only today, she couldn't dump a drink on the bitch and run out.

"How'd it go?" she asked.

ANDREA LAURENCE   115

Gavin settled Jared in his arms and turned to her. "Well, I think. They were surprised. Okay, *more* than surprised. But we talked a lot, and they've had some time to process it. Now I think they're excited at the prospect of their first grandchild."

It was too early for Sabine to feel optimistic. She was about to reply when she heard a woman's voice from inside the apartment. "Are they here? Ohmigosh, look at him!"

Sabine was expecting his mother, but instead, the face of a younger woman appeared over Gavin's shoulder. She had long, dark brown hair like his, but her eyes were a steely gray color. It had to be his sister, Diana.

Gavin turned toward her, showcasing his son. "This is Jared. Jared, this is your auntie Diana."

Jared played shy, turning his face into Gavin's shirt when Diana tried to coax him to say hello. More voices sounded inside with footsteps pounding across the floor. How many people were in there? A crowd of four or five people gathered, all fussing at Jared and Gavin at once.

"He looks just like you did at that age!"

"What a handsome boy!"

Sabine was happy to stay safely in the hallway and play spectator for the moment. It was easier. She always knew they would accept Jared. He was their blessed heir. The vessel that brought him into existence was another matter.

She could feel the moment the first set of eyes fell on her. It was Diana. She slipped around Gavin into the hallway, rushing Sabine with a hug she wasn't anticipating.

"It's so nice to finally meet you," Diana said.

Sabine patted weakly at the young woman's back and pulled away as soon as she could. "Finally?"

Diana smiled and threw a conspiratorial look over her shoulder. "Gavin had mentioned you to me when you were first dating. He just went on and on about you. I'd never heard him do that about another woman before. And then it ended and I was so disappointed. When he called and asked me to come over today to meet his son, I was so happy to hear that you were the mother." She grinned wide and nudged Sabine with her elbow. "I think it's fate."

Sabine tried not to laugh at the young woman's enthusiasm. She couldn't be more than twenty-two or twenty-three. She still believed in all that. And since Diana was the beautiful only daughter of a billion-dollar empire, Sabine was pretty certain no man had the nerve to break her heart. At least, not yet.

Diana snatched up Sabine's hand in hers and tugged her over the threshold of the entryway. The polished parquet floors were too slick for her to resist the movement and before she knew it, the door was closed and she was standing in the apartment of Byron and Celia Brooks.

Okay, apartment was a misnomer. This was a mansion slapped on the top of an apartment building. In front of her was a grand marble staircase with a gold-and-crystal chandelier twinkling overhead from the twenty-foot ceilings. On each side of the doorway were large urns filled with bouquets of fresh flowers that were nicer than the arrangements at some people's weddings.

That was all she could see with the press of people, but it was enough to let her know she wasn't in Nebraska anymore.

"Everyone, you remember Sabine Hayes. She's Jared's mother."

Sabine's chest tightened instantly, her breath going

still in her lungs of stone. Every eye in the room flew from Jared to her. His father's. His mother's. His brother Alan's. She tried to smile wide and pretend she wasn't having a panic attack, but she wasn't certain how convincing she was.

His mother stepped forward first. She looked just as she had the last time. Sabine and Gavin had run into them at a restaurant as they were going in and his parents were leaving. It had been an accidental meeting really, given their relationship hadn't called for the meeting of the parents yet. Sabine had been struck by how refined and effortlessly elegant his mother was. Today was no exception.

Celia's light brown hair was pulled back in a bun like Sabine's. She was wearing a gray silk dress with a strand of dark gray pearls around her neck and teardrops with diamonds from her ears. The dress perfectly matched her eyes, so much like Diana's. Her gaze swept quickly over Sabine from head to toe but stopped at her eyes with a smile of her own. "It's lovely to see you again, Sabine."

"Likewise," she said, politely shaking the woman's hand. Every description Gavin ever gave her of his mother had built an image of a cold, disinterested woman in Sabine's mind. Their meeting before hadn't been very revealing, but today, she instantly knew that was not the case. There was a light in her eyes that was very warm and friendly. Celia Brooks had just been raised well and taught early the rules of etiquette and civility that a woman of her class needed. Yes, she could've been a more hands-on mother and let her children get dirty every now and then, but that wasn't how she was brought up.

"Please, come in and meet everyone. You remember my husband, Byron, and this is my other son, Alan."

Sabine shook each of their hands and was amazed at how much alike the Brooks men looked. Thick brown hair, eyes like melted dark chocolate, strong builds. Just one glance and Sabine could tell exactly how Jared would look when he was twenty-five and when he was fifty-five.

"Nora has refreshments set up for us in the parlor," Celia said, ushering everyone out of the hallway.

The farther they went into the apartment, the more nervous Sabine became. Not because of his family, but because of their stuff. Every item her eyes lit upon looked fragile and priceless. "Do not put him down," Sabine whispered to Gavin.

At that, Gavin chuckled. "Do you have any idea how many things my siblings and I have broken over the years? I assure you, if it's important, it's not sitting out."

"Oh, yes," Celia insisted. "Don't worry about a thing. It has been quite a while since we had a youngster here, but we'd better get used to it, right?" She got a wistful look in her eye and glanced over at Jared. "A grandchild. What an unexpected and wonderful surprise."

Sabine wasn't quite sure what to say. She expected the other shoe to drop at any moment. But time went on, and it didn't. They chatted and nibbled on treats their housekeeper, Nora, made. His family asked questions about her with genuine interest. Jared was turned loose and managed not to break anything. To her shock, Byron, the former CEO of BXS, got on the floor and played with him and his dump truck.

She had made herself sick worrying about today. Thinking they would hate her. That they'd never accept her or her son. But as time went by, she found herself to be incredibly at ease with his family. They were polished and polite, but not cold and certainly not blatantly rude like Viola. It was nothing like she'd expected.

It seemed Sabine was as guilty of prejudice as she worried they would be. Just as she feared they would look at her and make snap judgments, so had she. She had this idea of what rich people were like. Gavin's stories of his distant, workaholic family had only reinforced the image in her mind.

But she was wrong. And it made her angry. People like Viola had made her believe that she could never have Gavin. That she would never fit in. She was angry at herself, really. She was the one who was too afraid to find out if their wicked whispers were true. She pushed away the only man she'd ever loved, deprived him of his son for two years, because she was certain they could never last.

She was wrong. At least in part. They might never truly be together as a couple again, but they could be a family and make it work.

Sabine had wasted so much time being afraid. She wasn't about to make the same mistake twice.

"You don't have to keep trying to take me out to dinner, Gavin."

"If at first you don't succeed, try, try again." Gavin smiled and helped her out of the car and onto the curb outside a restaurant.

"You didn't fail the last time." Sabine slowly approached him, pressed herself against the length of his body and wrapped her arms around his neck. "I seem to recall that evening ending in quite a…spectacular fashion."

"Spectacular, eh?" Gavin growled near her ear. "I'm

glad you seemed to think so. But—" he planted a kiss on her neck and whispered to her "—we never actually ate."

"That was okay with me." She looked up at him with her wide green eyes and a wicked smile curling her lips. "We could have the same thing tonight, if you'd like."

He smiled and let his hands roam across the silky fabric of her dress. She was trying to lure him back to bed, but he wouldn't let her. Couldn't let her. At least not tonight. "Well, as tempting as that is, I'll have to pass. You see, I brought in reinforcements to make sure this meal was a success. We can't stand up our guests."

Sabine frowned at him, her nose wrinkling. "Guests?"

"Sabine!"

She pulled away from Gavin and turned to find Adrienne and Will behind her. "Adrienne? Will? What are you two doing here?"

Adrienne leaned in to give her a hug with an amused smirk on her face. "Gavin invited us to have dinner with you tonight. Did he not tell you?"

"Uh, no, he didn't." Sabine looked over her shoulder at Gavin, who appeared appropriately admonished, at least for the moment. "How did you even know how to get in touch with either of them?"

"Gavin and I have been acquaintances for several years," Will said. "We play the occasional game of racquetball together."

Sabine just shook her head. "So…what? Do all young, rich guys know each other? Is there some kind of club or something where you all hang out and be rich together?"

"Yes, we have a support group—Rich and Sexy Anonymous," Gavin offered with a smile. "Let's get inside or we'll be late for our reservation."

They were seated at a table for four near the window.

He'd known Will for several years but hadn't connected that the Adrienne that Sabine worked for was the same Adrienne that married Will the year before. When the pieces finally clicked, he thought having dinner together would be nice. Not even Viola would have the nerve to come up to a table like this and make a fuss. They were guaranteed a fun night out with people that he already knew would make Sabine comfortable.

He had also been curious to meet Adrienne in person. He'd read about her in the newspaper a few years ago after her plane crash and the scandal that followed. She had lost her memory for weeks, and everyone thought she was Will's fiancée, who actually died in the wreck. It was the stuff of dramatic movies, but she had made herself into quite the success story. Her clothing line had soared in the past year, and her boutique was one of the most popular destinations for the young and hip in Manhattan. He just never thought to look for his runaway girlfriend behind the counter of the store.

The waiter came to take their drink orders. "Is anyone interested in some wine?"

"None for me," Adrienne said.

"We can order something sweeter," Sabine offered. "I know you like a Riesling or a Moscato, right?"

"I do normally—" she smiled "—but I'm not drinking at all for the next eight months or so."

The sharp squealing noise that followed was nearly enough to pierce Gavin's eardrums. Sabine leaped up from her chair and ran around to embrace Adrienne. That kicked off a rapid-fire female discussion about things that Gavin would rather not be privy to. Instead, he ordered sparkling water for Adrienne and wine for everyone else.

"Congrats, Daddy," he said to Will.

Will chuckled. "Congrats to you, as well. It seems to be going around."

"It has. I can assure you that mine was more of a surprise, since my child was walking and talking by the time I found out about it."

"Yeah, but you lucked out. You missed the morning sickness, the wild hormonal swings, the Lamaze classes, the birthing room where she threatens to castrate you. After the child is born there's the midnight feedings, the colic…"

Gavin listened to Will talk for a moment and shook his head to interrupt. "I'd gladly take all that and more in exchange for the rest of what I missed. I also didn't get to be there when she heard his heartbeat or saw his image on the sonogram for the first time. I missed his birth, his first steps, his first words…. Enjoy every moment of this experience with Adrienne. Things that don't seem very important now will be the very stuff that will keep you up at night when you're older. One day, you'll look up from your BlackBerry and your kid will be in high school."

Gavin couldn't stop the words from flying out of his mouth. Every single one of them was true, although he'd barely allowed himself the time to think about what he'd missed. He tried to focus on what was ahead. Jared wasn't going to drift in and out of his life like so many others, so he had no excuse. If he missed moments going forward, it was his own fault. He didn't want any more regrets.

The waiter brought their wine, and Gavin took a large sip. "Sorry about that," he said.

"No, don't be," Will answered. "You're right. Time goes by so quickly, especially to guys like us. The priorities start to change when you fall in love and even more so when kids come into the picture. I'll try to keep it in perspective when she's sending me out in the night on strange cravings runs."

"Gavin is taking us to look at apartments on my day off," he heard Sabine say.

"There's an apartment down the street from us that's for sale," Adrienne said. "A really nice brownstone. It's on the second floor, so there's some stairs, but not many."

"I think I'd prefer her to be in a building with a door-man and some security. It would make me feel better."

"It's not like my current apartment has surveillance cameras and security," Sabine said.

"It doesn't matter. If you continue to refuse living with me, I want you in someplace secure. I don't want just anyone strolling up to your door. This can be a dan-gerous town sometimes, and I want you and Jared pro-tected when I can't be there."

"Yes, that viciously dangerous Upper West Side," Sa-bine said with a smile. "I actually read that the Village has one of the higher crime rates, but you seemed okay with that."

"Hence the doorman."

"Okay, fine, no brownstones." The two women ex-changed knowing looks and shrugged.

They placed their orders and continued chatting eas-ily during the meal. Given they actually got as far as having food on the table, this was their most successful dinner yet. At this point, Gavin was thinking of opening a door to a line of conversation he was extremely inter-ested in. He hadn't brought it up to Sabine—she would likely shoot him down—but with Will and Adrienne as backup, he might be successful.

"So, are you guys planning to take any romantic pre-baby vacations sometime soon?"

The couple looked at each other. "That's not a bad idea," Will said. "We honestly haven't given it much thought. It really will be a challenge to travel with little ones. Honey," he said, turning to Adrienne, "we should definitely do something. Let's go somewhere glamorous and decidedly un-kid-friendly to celebrate. We're going to be making pilgrimages to the Mouse from now on, so we need to enjoy an adult vacation while we can."

"You really should," Sabine echoed. "That escape to your place in the Hamptons this summer was the only vacation I've taken since Jared was born. You should take the time to pamper yourself now. The spring lines are almost finished for Fashion Week. You should definitely go somewhere after the show."

Gavin perked up at her words. That was exactly what he was hoping to hear. "You've only had one vacation in two years?"

"More than that, really," she admitted. "Since I had Jared, I haven't had the time. Before I had Jared, I didn't have the money. Adrienne twisted my arm into going this summer. Prior to that, the last real vacation I took was my senior trip to Disney World in high school."

"That hardly counts," Will pointed out.

"Yes," Adrienne agreed. "You need a vacation as badly as I do. Maybe more. Thank goodness I got you to come to the beach house. I had no idea you were so vacation-deprived."

"I save all my hours in case Jared gets sick. And I don't have anyone to watch him while I'm gone. Tina had him over the Fourth of July trip, but I think that was too much for her. I couldn't ask her to do it again."

"You wouldn't have to," Gavin said.

"Are you offering to watch him while I go on vacation?" she challenged with a smile.

"Not exactly."

Nine

"This one is nice."

Sabine was gripping the handles of Jared's stroller as she shot him a glance that told him he was incorrect. She wasn't impolite enough to say that in front of the Realtor, though.

They were in the seventh apartment of the day. They had crisscrossed Manhattan, looking at places uptown, downtown, east and west. This last apartment, in midtown, had three spacious bedrooms, a large kitchen, a balcony and a spa tub in the master bath. And of course, it did not impress her nearly as much as some of the others. Unfortunately, it was the closest of all the apartments to his own place.

She favored the West Village, and there was no convincing her otherwise.

"This is probably a no," he said. "And I think we're

done for the day. The kid is getting tired." That was an understatement. He'd been conked out in his stroller since they arrived at this building.

"I really do like the one in the Village. I just want to know what all my options are before we spend that much. It's more than we need, really."

The woman sighed and closed her leather portfolio. "I'll keep looking and contact you next week with a list of other options. I worry you might lose out on that place if you don't put an offer in soon."

The Realtor was eyeing him from the other room. She was far too eager to push him into an expensive sale, and he wouldn't be rushed. Sabine would have what she wanted, and for the price he was willing to pay, this lady needed to find it for them.

"There are two million apartments in Manhattan," Gavin said. "We'll find another one if we have to."

They were escorted out of the apartment and downstairs. After they parted ways with the Realtor, they started strolling down the block. The street sounds roused Jared from his nap just as they neared Bryant Park.

"Could we take Jared over to the carousel? He loves that."

"Absolutely."

They took Jared for a spin on the carousel and then settled onto a bench to enjoy the nice afternoon. Gavin went to buy them both a drink, and when he returned, Jared was playing with another child who'd brought bubbles to the park.

"I've got a surprise for you."

Gavin had to smile at the mix of concern and intrigue on Sabine's face. He was excited about the prospect of what he had planned, but he also enjoyed watching her twist herself into knots trying to figure out what he was doing. She hated not knowing what was going on, which made him all the more determined to surprise her.

"Really?" Sabine turned away, feigning disinterest and watching Jared play with the bubbles.

It had been a couple days since she'd met his family. Things seemed to be going well on all fronts. Edmund said the custody and other legal paperwork should be finalized any day now. Gavin and his legal team were signing off on the merger agreement with Exclusivity Jetliners next week. Roger Simpson's son had finally stopped his loud protests about the acquisition, and things were moving forward.

Everything was going to plan, and Gavin wanted to celebrate the best way he knew how—an exhilarating flight and a luxurious weekend on the beach. For the first time in his life, he wanted to share that experience with someone else. He wanted Sabine beside him as he soared through the clouds and buried his toes in the sand. He just had to talk her into going along with it, which would be harder than securing an Exclusivity Jetliners jet and reserving a private beachfront bungalow in Bermuda on short notice.

"When you go home tonight, I want you to pack for a long weekend away."

Her head snapped back to look at him, a frown pulling down the corners of her pink lips. "I have to work this weekend, Gavin. I've already taken off too much time from the store. I can't go anywhere."

"Yes, you can," he said with a wide smile. Did she really think he would make a suggestion like this without having every detail handled? He ran an international shipping empire; he could manage taking her away for the weekend. "The lovely Adrienne and I spoke about my plans at dinner while you were in the ladies' room. She seemed very enthusiastic about it. You have the next three days off. She told me to tell you to have a good time and not to worry about anything."

Red rushed to Sabine's pale cheeks as her brow furrowed and she started to sputter. "What? You—y-you just went to my boss and made arrangements without asking me? Seriously? Gavin, you can't just make decisions like this and leave me out of them."

"Relax," he said, running a soothing hand over her bare shoulder. She was wearing a sleeveless blouse in a bright kelly green that made her eyes darken to the color of the oak leaves overhead. It was almost the same shade as when she looked at him with desire blazing in her eyes. "I'm not trying to take over your life. I'm just trying to take you on a little surprise getaway. You wouldn't do it if I didn't twist your arm."

His fingertips tingled as they grazed over her skin, rousing a need inside him that was inappropriate for the park. He hadn't made love to Sabine since they went to his apartment. She might have her concerns, but he was determined to take her to a tropical location where he could make love to her for hours, uninterrupted.

He wasn't sure whether it was his words or his touch, but the lines between her brows eased up. With a heavy sigh, she turned her attention back to the playground. "What will we do about Jared? You haven't mentioned him coming with us."

It was all handled. "My parents have volunteered to keep him for the weekend. They're quite excited about the prospect, actually."

Sabine's lips twisted as she tried, and failed, to hold in her concerns. "Your parents? The ones who left you with nannies, refused to let you get dirty or be loud or do anything remotely childlike? I don't see that going very well, to be perfectly honest."

Gavin shrugged. What was the worst that could happen? His parents had all the resources in the world at their fingertips. They could manage any contingency, even if it meant breaking down and hiring in someone to help them for the weekend. "I think it will be fine. This is completely different. From what I hear, being a grandparent has a different set of rules. They were distracted by work and responsibilities when I was a kid. Now, they've got nothing but time, cash and two years of indulging to catch up on. Worst-case scenario, we come home to a spoiled-rotten brat."

A soft chuckle escaped Sabine's lips as she turned back to the playground again. He followed her line of sight to the patch of grass where Jared and another little boy were chasing bubbles and giggling hysterically.

She was a great mother. She worried about their son and his welfare every second of the day and had done so for two straight years all on her own. A mother's protective nature never really went away, but Sabine needed a break. A weekend trip wouldn't hurt anything. In fact, she might come home refreshed and be a better parent for it.

"If it helps," Gavin added, "Nora, the housekeeper, used to work as a nanny. She's great with kids. If my parents need reinforcements, she'll be there to help. Nothing will go wrong. You deserve some time to relax."

"I don't know, Gavin. When you took him to the circus, I was nearly panicked the whole time. That was the first time he'd gone somewhere without me aside from day care. And now you want to take me on a trip? How far are we going?"

"Only a short plane ride away."

"Plane?" she cried, turning on the bench to face him full-on. "I really don't want to be that far from him, Gavin."

"It's only about a two-hour flight. If we drove to the Hamptons it would take just as long to get back home with summer traffic." He reached out and took her hand, relishing the cool glide of her skin against his. She had such delicate, feminine hands, more so than he remembered. He was used to them being rough with calluses from her wooden brushes, with paint embedded under her nails and along her cuticles. He hadn't managed to get her back to painting yet, but this trip was a sure start.

"Please let me do this for you. Not only will you have a great time, but it's my chance to share my passion with you the way you once shared your painting with me."

Her green eyes met his, and he felt some of her resistance fading away. She knew how important this was to him. "You're flying us there?"

Gavin smiled and nodded. It hadn't been an original part of his plan, but when he asked Roger about chartering one of his jets, he'd laughed and told him they were practically his already. If he wanted to take one, he was welcome to it, and he could fly it himself.

"Roger is loaning me one of his jets for the trip. I've been dying to fly one, and I really want you to be up there with me when I do. That would make the experience that much more special."

He loved to fly. Soaring through the air was the greatest high he'd ever experienced. It wasn't the same when you weren't sitting at the controls. The only thing that could make it better would be sharing it with her. Somehow, the idea of having Sabine beside him in the cockpit made his chest tight. He wanted to share this with her. He wanted to spoil her. She just had to let him.

She finally let the slightest smile curl her lips. He'd won, he could tell. The tiny smirk made him want to lean in and kiss her until she was blushing again, but this time with passion instead of irritation. But he'd have time soon enough. He wanted her in a swimsuit, her skin glistening with suntan oil. He couldn't wait to feel the press of her bikini bottom against him as he held her in the ocean. They both needed this trip away for a million different reasons.

"I suppose you're not going to tell me where we're flying to."

"Nope." He grinned.

"Then how do I know what to pack?"

"Dress for sizzling-hot days lounging on the beach and cool nights overlooking the ocean. Throw a couple things in a bag and leave the rest up to me."

Sabine wasn't a big fan of flying, but she wasn't about to tell Gavin that. It was his big love, like painting was for her, so she took her Dramamine, packed her bag and hoped for the best.

"You look nervous," Gavin said after locking the door and sliding into the cockpit beside her.

"Me?" she asked with a nervous twitter of laughter. "Never." She was thankful she'd worn large sunglasses today. Maybe he wouldn't notice her eyes were closed the whole time.

The taxi down the runway wasn't so bad. Gavin

seemed very at ease with his headset on and vast display of controls in front of him. He had given her a headset of her own to wear so she could hear the air traffic controllers talking. She heard the tower give them clearance to take off.

"Here we go," Gavin said with an impish smile that reminded her of Jared when he thought he was getting away with something naughty.

Gavin eased the accelerator forward and the jet started down the runway. At that point, Sabine closed her eyes and took a deep breath. She felt the lift as the plane surged into the sky, but she didn't open her eyes.

"Isn't it beautiful?" Gavin asked after a few minutes.

"Oh, yeah," she said, seeing nothing but the dark inside of her eyelids.

"Sabine, open your eyes. Are you afraid to fly?"

She turned to him with a sheepish smile. "No, I'm afraid to crash. You know my boss survived a plane crash a few years ago, right? When you know someone it happened to, it makes it more real in your mind." It was then that she looked through the glass and noticed nothing but ocean around them. He hadn't mentioned flying over the ocean. She swallowed hard. She could do this. She didn't really have a choice.

"We're not going to crash."

"No one plans to."

"Just breathe and enjoy the freedom of zooming through the sky like a bird. Soaring above everyone and everything."

She pried her gaze away from the vast stretch of ocean that surrounded them and decided to focus on Gavin instead. His eyes were alight with excitement. Her serious businessman was grinning from ear to ear like a child with his first bicycle. He adjusted the controls like a pro, setting the cruising altitude and putting them on a course to...*somewhere.*

It was an amazing transformation. Sabine had seen Gavin happy. Angry. Sad. She'd watched his face contort in the pinnacle of passion and go blank with deep thought. But not once had she ever seen him truly joyful. It suited him. He should've joined the Air Force. He might not have a thirty-million-dollar apartment on Central Park South, but he would've been happier. Sometimes you have to make the hard choices to chase your dream. She'd left her entire family behind to follow hers and had rarely regretted the decision.

Two hours later, Gavin started talking into the headset again, and they were granted permission to land although she didn't see anything but miles of blue sea. The plane slowly dropped in altitude. The ocean lightened to a bright turquoise blue, and mossy-green islands appeared through the clouds. She closed her eyes when they landed, but Gavin did a great job at that.

They taxied around the small island airport, finally passing a sign to help her figure out where she was. Welcome to Bermuda.

Bermuda!

At the hangar, they were directed to a location to leave the jet. Gavin shut all the equipment down and they opened the door, extending steps to the ground. Sabine was excited about the trip but grateful to finally have her sandals touching the earth again.

Gavin directed a couple men to unload luggage from the cargo hold and move it to a black town car waiting outside. The driver then whisked them through the narrow, winding streets. After a while, they turned off the main road to a sand-and-gravel drive that disappeared through the thick cover of trees. The world seemed to slip farther away with every turn until at last they came upon a secluded two-story home right on the beach. The house was bright yellow with a white roof and white shutters around each window.

The driver carried their bags inside, leaving them on the tile floor of the master bedroom suite. Sabine followed behind him, taking in every detail of their home away from home. It was decorated in a casual beach style with bright colors and lots of light. There were large French doors off the living room that opened onto a deck. She walked outside, stepping onto it and realizing that it actually extended out over the water.

Sabine leaned against the railing and looked all around her. She didn't see another house or boat anywhere. There was nothing but palm trees, black volcanic rock, clear blue water and pink sand. It was unexpected, but peachy-pink sand stretched out on either side of them.

"The sand is pink," she said, when she heard Gavin step out onto the patio behind her.

"I thought you'd like that." He pressed against her back and wrapped his arms around her waist.

Sabine sighed and eased against him. She could feel the tension start to drift away just being here in his arms. He was right. As much as she'd protested, she needed this vacation.

"I didn't even know such a thing existed. It's beautiful." Her gaze fell on some multicolored glittering stones in the sand. "What is that?" She pointed to the beach. "Shells?"

"Sea glass. They have some beaches here that are just covered in it."

Sabine had the urge to walk along the beach and collect some glass to take home. Maybe she could work it into her art. She hadn't done any painting yet, but she had begun allowing herself to think about it again. The ideas were forming, waiting for her to execute when she was ready. Sea glass might very well feature prominently in the first piece.

"This place is amazing. I want to paint it."

Gavin nuzzled his nose along the shell of her ear. "Good. I want you to paint. I even brought supplies with me."

Sabine turned in his arms with a small frown. "I didn't notice any canvases."

He grinned and planted his hands on the railing to trap her there. "That's because they're body paints. I'm your canvas."

"Oohhh…" Sabine cooed, the possibilities flowing into her mind. This could certainly be fun. "When can we start my next masterpiece?"

Gavin captured her lips with his own, coaxing her blood to move faster and her skin to flush with the heat of desire. One hand moved to her waist and slid beneath her shirt to caress her bare skin. "Right now," he whispered against her lips.

He took her hand and led her back inside. In the bedroom, his luggage was open, and sitting on the dresser was a box of body paints. Gavin must've unpacked it after their driver left. She picked up the pink box and eyed it with curiosity. "You didn't mention it was edible."

"I thought it might bother you to destroy your own creation."

Sabine pulled a jar of strawberry-flavored red paint

from the box with a wicked grin. "Given I'd be destroying it with my tongue, I don't mind so much."

She advanced toward the bed, Gavin stepping backward until his calves met with the mattress. Sabine set down the paints long enough to help him slip out of his clothes and lie out on the king-size bed.

There wasn't anything quite as inspirational as seeing his powerful, naked body sprawled in front of her. His arms were crossed behind his head, his rock-hard chest and chiseled abs just waiting for her artistic improvements. This was an exciting new canvas, and unlike the one he brought to her apartment, there was no blank, white surface to mock her.

Easing onto the bed beside him, she arranged her jars and pulled out the brush that came with it. It wasn't exactly the highest-quality equipment, but this wasn't going to hang in the Louvre one day.

Thinking for a moment, she dipped the brush into the blueberry paint and started swirling it around his navel. He hissed for a moment at the cold paint and then smiled. Next, she added some strawberry paint. Then green watermelon and purple grape. She lost herself in the art, mixing the colors around his skin until he looked like her own twisted, edible version of an abstract Kandinsky painting.

After nearly an hour, she sat back on her heels and admired her canvas. She liked it. It really was a shame it wouldn't last through his next shower.

"I like watching you work."

Sabine turned to look at him, his face one of the only parts of his body that didn't look like a unicorn had thrown up a rainbow on him. "Thanks."

"You get this intensity in your eyes that's amazingly

sexy." He sat up to admire his body. "I can say with certainty that this is probably the greatest abstract art piece ever created with edible body paints. And," he added with a grin, "the only one that smells like a bowl of Froot Loops."

She reached out with her brush and dabbed a dot of purple paint on his lips, then leaned in to lick it away. Her tongue glided slowly along his bottom lip, her gaze never leaving his. "Tasty."

He buried his fingers in her hair and tugged her mouth back to his. His tongue dipped inside and glided along her own. "Indeed. The grape is very tasty."

Sabine smiled and pushed him back against the bed. "That was fun, but now it's time to clean up."

She started with his chest, licking a path across his pecs and flicking her tongue across his nipples. She made her way down the flavorful canvas, teasing at his rib cage and the sensitive plane of his stomach. When she glanced up, she noticed Gavin watching just as eagerly as when she was painting.

"I told you I liked watching you work," he said with a grin.

Sabine dipped lower to the firm heat of his erection and wiped away his smile with her tongue. Taking it deep into her mouth, she worked hard to remove every drop of paint, leaving Gavin groaning and clutching at the blankets with his fists.

"Sabine," he whispered, reaching for her wrist. He found her and tugged until her body was sprawled across his. "You're wearing too much clothing," he complained.

Sitting astride him, Sabine slipped out of her top and bra and then stood to push down her capris and panties. She tossed everything onto the floor and crouched back down. With little effort, she was able to take him into her body and thrust him deep inside.

His hands moved quickly to her hips, guiding her movements. Sabine closed her eyes and tried to absorb the sensations, but found that without the distraction of painting, her emotions were starting to creep in.

From the moment he first kissed her, Sabine had worried that she was fighting a losing battle. Not for custody of Jared, but for custody of her heart. No matter how many times she told herself that none of this was about them, that it was about his son, she couldn't help but think it was more.

Sure, everything he offered would make her a happier mother for their child. But he didn't need to bring her here, to make love to her like this. He didn't have to be so supportive of her art when no one else was. It made it seem like more. And she wanted it to be more. She was just afraid.

Sabine loved him. She always had. There were plenty of reasons why they wouldn't make a good couple, but in the end, only one reason mattered. She left because she loved him enough to change for him—the one thing she swore she'd never do. She'd been disowned by her family for her unwillingness to bend, and yet she would be whatever Gavin wanted her to be. And it scared the hell out of her. So she made her excuses and ran before she did something she might hate herself for.

There was no running from Gavin now. He would forever be a part of her life. And she didn't have the strength to keep fighting this. He might never love her the way she loved him. But she couldn't pretend that this meant nothing to her.

Gavin groaned loudly, pulling her from her thoughts. He moved his hand up to cup her breast, the intensity of their movements increasing with each moment that went by. She wouldn't be able to hold out much longer.

Opening her eyes, she looked down at Gavin. His eyes were closed, his teeth biting down on his lip. He was completely wrapped up in his desire for her. For *her*. Just the way she was. He'd told her that the night she fought with Viola, but she wasn't ready to listen. Perhaps he really meant it. Perhaps he wouldn't ask her to change and she wouldn't betray how weak she was by giving in to his demands.

Perhaps one day he might love her for being herself.

That thought made her heart soar with hope and her body followed. The pleasure surged through her, her cries echoing in the large, tile-floored room. Gavin quickly followed, digging his fingers into the flesh of her hips and growling with satisfaction.

When their heartbeats slowed and they snuggled comfortably into each other's arms, Sabine spoke. Not the words she wanted to say, but the ones she needed to say. "Thank you."

"For what?"

"For the paint. And all of this, really. But mostly the paint."

"I assure you, the pleasure was all mine."

Sabine laughed and nestled tighter against his still somewhat rainbow-colored chest. "That's not what I meant. You've always been such a big supporter of my work. I haven't…" Her voice trailed off as tears crept into her words. She cleared her throat. "I haven't always had that in my life.

"After I had Jared and stopped painting, I began to worry that I might lose my touch. When you brought that canvas the other day and the ideas didn't come, I was really worried my art career was done. Today showed me that I still have the creativity inside me. I just need to not put so much pressure on myself and have fun with it again. It doesn't seem like much, but those body paints were a big deal. For me."

"I'm glad," Gavin said, holding her tight. "I have to say it's the best fifteen bucks I've ever spent at the adult novelty store."

Ten

"We should really call and check in on Jared."

Gavin tugged her tight against him and shook his head. They had made love, showered off her artwork, eaten—as body paints are not a replacement for real food—made love again and taken a nap. He wasn't anywhere near ready to let go of her. Not even just so she could grab her phone from the other room.

"I told my parents to call if there was a problem. I want you one hundred percent focused on enjoying yourself and relaxing. They've got it under control. We've only been gone for eight hours."

He could feel her start to squirm, but he wasn't budging. "How about we call in the morning?"

"Okay. I'm sure everything's fine, but I'm just a nervous mama. I worry."

"I know. But remember, our parents raised us, at least

yours did. Mine hired very qualified people to do it. They know what they're doing."

"I'd rather you not use my parents as an example of good parenting."

Gavin had never heard Sabine speak at length about her family or where she grew up. He knew it was some-where in the Midwest, but she always seemed hesitant to talk about it. Since she opened the door, he'd take the opportunity. "Do your parents know about Jared?"

He felt Sabine stiffen in his arms. "No," she finally said.

"Why not?"

She wiggled until he allowed her to roll onto her back and look at him. "They are very religious, very hard-working Midwestern farmers. They worship God, the Cornhuskers and John Deere, in that order. I grew up in a small town that was nothing but cornfields and the occasional church for miles. From the time I was a teen-ager, I started to divert from the path they all followed. My parents tried their hardest to guide me back, but it didn't work. They decided they didn't want anything to do with me and this crazy life I wanted to lead. I refuse to expose Jared to grandparents that would just look at him as my shameful illegitimate son that my wild city life earned me."

"What happened between you and your family?" Gavin asked.

Sabine sighed, her kiss-swollen lips pursing in thought. She didn't really want to talk about it, but she needed to and they both knew it.

"Like I said, I wasn't the child they wanted. I wasn't willing to change who I was or what I dreamed of for them. They wanted me to be a quiet, mousy girl that would get up at dawn to cook for my husband and the other farmhands, take care of a brood of children and be content to sit on the porch and snap green beans. My two sisters didn't see anything wrong with that, but it wasn't what I wanted for my life. They couldn't understand why I wanted a nose ring instead of a wedding ring. The first time I dyed my bangs pink, my mother nearly had a heart attack. My art, my dreams of New York and being a famous painter…that was all childish nonsense to them. They wanted me to 'grow up' and do something respectable."

Gavin knew what it was like not to have his family support his choices. But he hadn't been brave like Sabine. He'd caved to the pressure. He envied her strength, especially knowing the high price she'd paid for her dreams. She had no contact with her family at all?

"You don't even speak to your sisters, then?"

"Very rarely. They're both older than I am, but the younger of the two talks to me on Facebook now and then. When we do talk, it's like chatting superficially with an old friend from junior high you barely remember. We don't share much. I don't post anything about Jared online, so none of them know about him. It seems that when I refused the life they chose I was insulting them, too. In trying to make myself happy, I made everyone else mad."

"So how did you end up in New York?"

"After graduation, I was toying with the idea of leaving Nebraska. I was working as a checkout girl at the grocery store and hoarding every penny I made. My parents had started this ridiculous parade of eligible farmers through the house each week at Sunday dinner just like they had with my older sisters. I could feel my opportunity to leave slipping away. If I wasn't careful, eventually one of the men would catch my eye. Then I'd end up pregnant or married, and I'd never get to New York.

"One night, after I walked the latest guy out, I returned to the living room and announced to my parents that I was moving out. I'd finally saved up enough to get there and a little money to live on. I told them I had a bus ticket to Manhattan and I would be leaving in the morning. It scared the daylights out of me, but I had to do it."

Gavin noticed the faint shimmer of tears in her eyes. The room was dark, but there was enough moonlight to catch it. Her parents hurt her and he hated them for it. "What did they say when you told them?"

She didn't reply right away. When she finally spoke, the tears had reached her voice, her words wavering with emotions. "They said to go on and go, then. Why wait for the morning? My dad grabbed the bag I had packed and threw it in the back of his truck."

Sabine sniffed delicately and wiped her eyes. "They were done with me. If I wasn't going to be the daughter they wanted me to be, then I just wouldn't be their daughter. My mama didn't say a word. She just shook her head and went to do the dishes. That's all she ever did was clean that damned kitchen. So I climbed into the truck and left. I wasn't even finished packing, but I couldn't make myself go upstairs to get the last of my things. I ended up sleeping in the bus station that night because I couldn't change my ticket."

"Just like that?"

"Just like that." She sighed, pulling her emotions back into check. "They disowned me. I don't know if they secretly thought I would fail and come running home, or if they were just tired of dealing with my eccentricities.

I wasn't the town tramp. I wasn't pregnant or on drugs. I was smart, I graduated high school with good grades. I worked and did my share around the farm. But I didn't fit this mold they tried to force me into.

"That was the last time I saw or spoke to my parents. The saddest part is that despite the fact that I wanted to go, I wanted them to ask me to stay. But they didn't. They just let me walk out like I meant nothing to them."

Gavin felt a sick knot start to form in his stomach. He'd done the exact same thing to her. All this time, he'd only focused on the fact that Sabine had left like everyone else in his life. He'd never considered that she might stay if he'd asked. And he'd wanted to. Every nerve in his body was screaming for him to say something—do *something*—to keep Sabine from leaving him, but he'd sat quietly and let her walk away.

"You know, people make mistakes. I'm willing to bet that they love you and miss you. Maybe they thought they were giving you one of those hard life lessons thinking you would come back and be more grateful for what you had. And when you didn't…they didn't know what to do. Or how to find you."

"I'm not that hard to find. Like I said, I'm on Facebook. For a while, I even had a website for my art."

Gavin shook his head. "It's not always as easy as that, especially when you know you're in the wrong. I mean, I did the same thing, didn't I? I was stupid and stubborn and let you walk away. I had a million idiotic reasons for it at the time, but none of them held up the moment that door slammed. Whenever I think back on that day, I wonder what would've happened if I'd run after you. If I'd pulled you into my arms and told you that I needed you to stay."

"You wanted me to stay?"

There was such astonishment in her voice that made him feel even worse. She thought he didn't care. All this time. A part of her probably still did. He hadn't asked for more than her body. Perhaps that's all she thought he wanted. It was all he thought he wanted, until this moment.

"Of course I wanted you to stay. I was just so caught off guard. I had let myself believe that you were different, that you wouldn't leave because you cared about me. When you broke it off, my world started to crumble. I just didn't know how to ask you to stay. You know that I'm not good with that kind of thing. Feelings..." His voice drifted off as he shook his head. He sucked at the emotional stuff.

"It's easier than you think."

Gavin planted a kiss against the crown of her head. "It is?"

"Yes." She propped up onto one elbow and looked him in the eyes. "All you had to say is 'stay.' Just that one word is enough."

"If I had said it the day you left..." He hated to ask, but he had to know.

"I would have stayed."

Gavin swallowed hard and nodded. So many people had come and gone from his life. How many of them might still be around if he'd had the nerve to ask them to stay? Some things were out of his control, but at least he could've salvaged the past few years with Sabine.

It was hard to face the fact that one little word could've changed their entire lives. But sometimes that was all it took. He looked down at the beautiful woman in his arms, the mother of his child, and he vowed he would never let something that insignificant get in the way again.

* * *

Sabine stretched out on the lounge chair and sighed. Gavin was snoozing in the chair beside her as they both soaked in the warm sunshine and light breeze. She was really enjoying this little vacation. They had eaten too much, drank too much, slept late and made love more times than she could count. Gavin had even taken her to the Bermuda Botanical Gardens and the art museum there. She'd lost herself in room after room of paintings and sculptures, lighting the fires of her long-cold creative flames.

It was all too perfect.

She couldn't believe how wrong she'd been. About everything. From the day she took that first pregnancy test, she worried that Gavin would take over her life, steal her son and leave her powerless to stop him. So far, he'd wanted to help, wanted to have his time with his son, but had respected her boundaries. Things would change, but they would compromise on the decisions. There would be no boarding schools, no nannies taking the place of loving parents...

She'd thought Gavin didn't want her, only to find out he'd been devastated when she left. He hadn't told her that he loved her, but she could tell he had feelings for her. They might not be as strong as what she felt for him, but it was more than she ever expected to have.

She thought that she would never fit into Gavin's world or be the woman he wanted her to be. Now, she realized he didn't want her to fit in. He wanted her to be herself. There would always be people with something rude to say, but if his family welcomed her with open arms, she didn't really care what anyone else thought.

Things were going amazingly well.

A soft chirp distracted Sabine from her thoughts. It was Gavin's cell phone. It had been remarkably quiet since they'd arrived. He'd done well in focusing on their vacation, too. She watched him reach for it and frown at the screen before answering.

"Hi, Dad," he said. "Is everything okay?"

Immediately, Sabine's stomach sank. They had called yesterday to check in and everything was fine. He'd told her that his parents would only call if there was a problem. She tried to will herself to relax as she listened to half of the conversation.

"What?" Gavin's tone was sharp and alarmed. He shot up on the lounge chair, his worried gaze searching the ocean for answers he wouldn't find there. "Are you sure? Did you look in all the closets and under the beds? He likes to play hide-and-seek."

Sabine sat up in her chair, swinging her legs over the side to turn toward him. "What is it? Is Jared okay?"

Gavin wouldn't look at her. He was totally focused on the call. "How did they get in the apartment?"

They? Her heart was racing.

"Did you call the police?"

"Gavin!" Sabine cried, unable to stand not knowing what was going on any longer. If Jared fell and skinned his knee, the police wouldn't be involved. This was something far worse than she could imagine.

"No, that was the right thing to do. We'll be home in three hours." Gavin turned off his phone and finally looked at her. He had the shimmer of glassy tears in his eyes as he spoke. "Jared is gone."

A strangled cry escaped her throat. "Gone? He's missing? How?"

Gavin shook his head softly. "Not missing. Kidnapped. A ransom note was left."

Sabine's brain started to swim in panic. She could barely follow his words. She couldn't possibly have heard him right. No one would take Jared. Why would anyone take Jared? "What?" she said, but she couldn't understand his answer. Nothing made sense.

Gavin stood up and offered his hand to her, but she didn't know why. "Sabine, please," he said at last. "We have to get back to New York."

She took his hand, standing slowly until she was looking into his eyes. His eyes. Just like her son's. That's when the fog in her brain cleared, and all that was left behind was red fury.

Her baby had been taken. Her sweet little boy, who had been nothing but safe under her care. Until now. Until he became the son of one of the wealthiest men in Manhattan. Then he was just a pawn in the games of the rich.

"Sabine?"

Her gaze locked on his, her lips tightening with anger. Gavin reached out to touch her face, but she swatted his hand away. "Don't you touch me," she warned through gritted teeth. "This is all your fault."

It was as though she'd slapped him across the face. He flinched and stepped back. "What?"

"I never should've listened to you. You said he would be safe with your parents."

"Of course. Why would I think someone would kidnap our son?"

"Because that's the world you live in, Gavin. You might be appalled by the way we lived with our tiny apartment and our old, worn furniture, but you know what? Jared was safe! He was a safe, happy little boy who didn't know what he was missing. And now he's a rich little boy, scared and alone because being *your son* made him a target."

"You think I'm the reason he was kidnapped?"

There was hurt in Gavin's eyes, but she ignored it. She was too deep in her rage to care. "You are *absolutely* the reason he was kidnapped. What did the ransom note say? Did they want millions of dollars? They wouldn't have gotten that from me, no matter what. I have nothing to offer, nothing anyone could possibly want, unlike you."

"I don't know what the ransom note said aside from the fact that they would call with instructions at 5:00 p.m. If we leave now, we can get back in plenty of time. Can you stop yelling long enough to pack and get on the plane?"

"You bet I can. I don't want to be on the island with you for another minute anyway." Sabine spun on her heel and ran from him, kicking pink sand as she headed for the stairs. She leaped up them two at a time until she reached the deck and raced for the master bedroom.

"What is that supposed to mean?" he said, charging in behind her.

"It means I wish I'd never run into Clay on the street. That the last two weeks had never happened. I should've gone home to Nebraska so you could never find me. If you weren't a part of Jared's life, I would have my son with me right now. This is exactly why I didn't tell you that you were a father."

The hurt expression on Gavin's face quickly morphed into anger. His dark eyes narrowed dangerously at her. "That is a load of crap and you know it. You didn't tell me about Jared because you're a control freak who couldn't stand someone else being involved in decisions for *your* son. You didn't tell me because you're selfish and you wanted him all to yourself, no matter what the cost to him."

"You bastard! I was protecting him from the life you hated."

"Yes, because it was so much better to suffer for your child and get sympathy than to give up your child dictatorship. Martyrdom doesn't look good on you, Sabine."

Her cheeks flushed red with anger. She didn't know what to say to him. There wasn't anything else to say. She turned her back on him and focused on packing and getting home to her son. She threw open her bag and chucked everything within reach into it. Whatever was too far away wasn't important enough to worry about. By the time she had her things together, so did he. He was standing at the front door, a car waiting for them in the driveway.

She couldn't speak. If she opened her mouth, she would say more horrible things. Some she meant, some she didn't. It was probably the same for him. Yelling made her feel better when she felt so helpless. Instead, she brushed past him to the car, giving her bags over to the driver and climbing inside.

The ride to the airport was just as silent. Her anger had begun to dissipate; this wasn't the time to start blaming and arguing. That time would come later, when Jared was home safely and she could think of something, anything, but her son's welfare.

The plane was well on its way back to New York before she so much as looked in Gavin's direction. There was only a foot between them, but it could've been miles. "Listen, fighting isn't going to get us anywhere, so let's call a truce until this whole mess is over."

Gavin's fingers flexed around the controls with anger

and anxiety, but the plane didn't so much as waver under his steady command. "Agreed."

"What else did your parents say when they called?"

"They had taken him to the park and then brought him home to take a nap before lunch. My mother said she fell asleep herself on the chaise in the living room. When she got up to check on him, he was gone and the ransom note was left on the bed."

"No one else was home?"

"My father was in his office. Nora had gone out to pick up groceries."

Sabine shook her head and focused her gaze on the miles of ocean between her and her baby. "How can someone just walk into a multimillion-dollar apartment building and walk out with our son? Did no one see him? Not even the doorman? Surely there are cameras everywhere."

"Whoever it was didn't go through the front door. They probably went in through the parking garage. There are cameras all over, but it requires a police request for them to pull the surveillance tapes."

"And?"

"And," Gavin said with a heavy sigh, "we haven't called the cops yet. The note threatened Jared's safety if we involved the police. I want to wait and take the kidnapper's call tonight. Then we might have a better idea of who we're working with here. At that point, we might get the NYPD to come in."

Sabine wasn't sure if she liked this plan or not. This was her first involvement with a kidnapping outside episodes of *Law & Order,* but calling the cops always seemed to be step number one in those situations. But perhaps Gavin had more insight into this than he was sharing. "You said 'a better idea of who we're working with.' Do you know who might be involved in this?"

Gavin shrugged, the dismissive gesture making her angrier than she already was. "It might not be anyone I know. With this kind of thing, it could just be some random creep out to make a quick buck in ransom money. You were right to say that claiming my son made him a target. It did. I hadn't really considered that until now.

"But I can't help but think this is someone I know. Jared isn't common knowledge yet. I can't be certain, but I've got a pretty short suspect list. Despite what you might think, I don't go around ruining my competitors and giving them reason to hate me."

"Who, out of those people, would despise you enough to kidnap your son?"

"Three, tops. And that's a stretch."

"And how many," Sabine asked with a tremble in her voice, "would be willing to *kill* your son for revenge?"

Gavin turned and looked at her, the blood draining from behind his newly tanned skin. "No one," he said, although not with enough confidence to make her feel better. "No one."

Eleven

Truthfully, Gavin only had one suspect on his list. As the time drew close for the call from the kidnappers, he was fairly certain who would be on the other end.

They had arrived safely at the airport and made their way to his parents' apartment as quickly as they could. His parents looked nearly ill when they walked in. His father's larger-than-life confidence had crumbled. His mother looked paper-thin and fragile. This had shaken them and it was no wonder. Their home, the one they'd shared for over thirty years, had been tainted by someone bold enough to stroll inside and walk out with the most precious treasure in their possession.

Sabine and his mother hugged fiercely and then went to sit together on the couch. His father paced in the corner, staring out the window at the city that had somehow betrayed him. Nora brought a tray with hot tea and nibbles that no one could stomach touching. Gavin just sat and waited for the call.

When the phone finally rang, Gavin's heart leaped into his throat. He answered on the second ring, gesturing for silence in the room. They had not called the police, but if the four nervous adults swarming him weren't quiet, the kidnapper might think the mansion was overrun with investigators and hostage negotiation teams.

"Hello?" he choked out.

"Gavin Brooks," the man said with an air of confidence that bordered on arrogance. Gavin didn't recognize the voice, but he hadn't spoken to his primary suspect. "So glad you could come home from your luxury vacation for our little chat."

"I want to talk to Jared," Gavin demanded as forcefully as he could.

Sabine leaped up and sat beside him on the couch. They hadn't really spoken much since their fight, and things might be irrevocably broken between them, but in this moment, they were united in finding their son and making sure Jared returned home safe and sound. He reached out and took her trembling hand in his. He was just as nervous, just as scared as she was, but he was better at not showing it. Holding her hand and keeping her calm was like an anchor on his own nerves. It kept the butterflies in his stomach from carrying him off into the sky.

"I bet you do. But you're not in charge here. I am. And you've got a couple hoops to jump through before that's even on the table."

"How do I know that you really have him?"

"If I don't…who does? You haven't misplaced your son, have you?"

"Is he okay?"

"For now. I haven't harmed a hair on his handsome little head. If you want to keep it that way, you'll do exactly as I ask and not involve the police. If you call the cops, we're done negotiating and you'll never see your little boy again."

Gavin nervously squeezed Sabine's hand. She smiled weakly at him, confusing his gesture as one of reassurance. He felt anything but sure. "I'm not calling the police. I want to keep this between you and me. But I have to know. What, exactly, do you want, Paul?"

The man on the other end of the line chuckled bitterly. "Aww, shoot. I was hoping it would take longer for you to figure out who was behind this. How did you guess it was me? I thought you'd be ruining the lives of half a dozen people right now, but you narrowed the field pretty quickly."

Paul Simpson. He had been right on the money with his original guess. Roger's irresponsible only son was the heir to Exclusivity Jetliners. At least until his father signed over the company to Gavin on Tuesday. The looming deadline must have pushed Paul too far. He had no choice but to act. That left little question of what his ransom demand would be.

"Only a handful of people knew I was going out of town. Even fewer knew that I had a son. That's not common knowledge yet."

Gavin had mentioned the trip to Roger when they spoke on the phone Thursday. He'd mentioned taking Sabine to Bermuda and that his parents would be watching Jared. That's when Roger had graciously offered the jet. If Paul was listening in on their conversation, all he had to do was wait for the right moment to slip in and steal away their son. He had handed his enemy the ammunition to attack him and didn't even realize it.

The only plus to this scenario was that Paul was spineless. Or so he seemed. Roger didn't have much faith in his son. When he snapped, Paul jumped to attention. That said, Gavin wouldn't have given him the credit to plan a scheme like this, so maybe he was wrong. He wouldn't push Paul to find out.

"Ahh. Well, mistakes are bound to be made in a scenario like this. Fortunately, we don't have to worry about any of that because this is going to go smoothly and without issue."

Somehow, Gavin doubted it. "What do you *want,* Paul? You still haven't told me what you're after with all this, although I have a pretty good guess."

"It's simple, really. First, you're going to call my father. You tell him that you have to back out of the merger deal. Give him whatever excuse you want to. Aside from blackmail, of course. But end it, and now."

The sinking feeling in his gut ached even more miserably than it had before. His dream of having his own jet fleet was slipping through his fingers. Everything he'd worked for, everything he'd built toward in the past few years would be traded away for his son. Gavin hadn't been a father for long, but he would do anything to keep Jared safe. If that meant losing Exclusivity Jetliners, that was the price he would pay. But that didn't mean it wouldn't hurt.

He should've seen this coming. Paul had silenced his complaints about the sale recently. Roger had thought that he had finally convinced his son to see reason, but the truth was that Paul was quietly looking into alternatives to get his way. Going around his father was the best plan. But it wouldn't solve all of his problems.

"If I don't buy the company, your father will just sell it to someone else."

"No!" Paul shouted into the line. "He won't. If this falls through, he'll give me the chance to try running the company on my own. Then I can prove to him that I can do it and he won't sell."

Gavin wanted to tell Paul he was delusional, but he couldn't. The moment Jared was safely in his arms, he'd have the NYPD swarming this guy and hauling his ass to Rikers Island for the foreseeable future. He wouldn't be running a company anytime soon.

"After I call Roger and cancel the deal, we get our son back?"

"Not exactly," Paul chuckled. "First, I have to confirm with my father that the merger is out for good. After that, I need a little financial insurance. I expect to see you at the bank bright and early in the morning—and yes, I am watching you. You'll withdraw a million in small bills and put it into a backpack. I'll call again in the morning with the rendezvous point."

"And then we get Jared back."

"And then," Paul sighed in dismay, "yes, you get your precious little boy back. But first, phone my father and call off the deal. I'll be calling him in half an hour, and I expect him to share the disappointing news when I speak to him. You'll hear from me at 10:00 a.m. tomorrow."

The line went dead.

Gavin dropped the phone onto the table and flopped back into the cushions of his couch. He was fighting to keep it together, but inside, it felt as if his world was crumbling. His son was in danger. The one person he believed was in his life for good could be permanently snatched away on the whim of a ruthless man. His dreams of owning private jets were about to be crushed. The woman he cared for blamed him for all of it and might never forgive him if something went wrong. She was already one foot out of his life, he could tell.

But nothing he could say or do would guarantee that Jared would be handed over, unharmed. Or that Sabine would ever look at him with love in her eyes again.

She was watching him silently from the seat beside him. He was still clutching her hand, worried if he let go, he'd lose her forever. "Well," she said at last. "What did you find out?"

"Is Jared okay?" his mother asked.

"Yes, I think so. I know who has orchestrated this and why. I don't have any reason to believe that he won't return Jared to us safe and sound as long as I meet his demands."

She breathed a visible sigh of relief. "Who has him?"

"Paul Simpson. No one you know."

"What did he ask for?" His father finally entered the conversation.

"A million-dollar ransom, delivered tomorrow in exchange for Jared."

"Our accountant can make that happen," Byron confirmed.

"And today," Gavin continued, "the cancellation of my latest business deal."

Sabine gasped and squeezed his hand even tighter. "The one you were working with the private jet company?"

Gavin nodded, his gaze dropping down to his lap.

"Yes. I hope you enjoyed riding in that plane to Bermuda. That will probably be the last time."

"Oh, Gavin, I'm so sorry." Her pale eyes, lined with worry, were at once glassy with tears. For a moment he was jealous that she could cry for what he was losing and he couldn't. "I know how important that was to you. Maybe you can still—"

Gavin pulled his hand away and held it up to silence her. He wasn't in the mood to deal with the maybes and other consolations she could offer. It wouldn't matter. "Even if this all works out, I think my dealings with the Simpson family are over."

"We can acquire more planes, son."

He shook his head at his father. "Finding another company with a quality fleet I can afford is nearly impossible. The shareholders won't back a more expensive merger. The whole concierge plan is dead."

He turned away from his family and picked up his phone. He needed to call Roger, but that would wait a few more minutes. More important was calling his accountant. He didn't exactly leave thousands of dollars just lying around, much less a million. Some things would need to be shifted around so he had liquid assets for the ransom. His accountant would get everything together for him with little fuss.

The awkward call to his accountant took only a few minutes. The man seemed confused by the sudden and out-of-ordinary request, but he didn't question it. The money would be ready for pickup in the morning. That done, he couldn't put off the inevitable any longer.

Gavin slowly dialed the familiar number of Roger Simpson. With every fiber of his being, he didn't want to back out of this deal. It was everything he'd desired, and it was mere days from being his at last. He wasn't even sure how he would say the words out loud. His tongue might not cooperate. He'd rather shout at Roger about how his son was volatile, if not plain disturbed. But he wouldn't. Not while Jared's life was in another person's hands.

"Gavin?" Roger answered. "I didn't expect to hear from you today. You're back early from Bermuda. Did something happen? Was something wrong with the jet I loaned you?"

"The jet was fine. Don't worry about any of that. Something came up and we had to come back ahead of schedule." He just couldn't tell him that the something involved blackmail and kidnapping. "I—I'm sorry to have to make this call, Roger. I'm afraid I have to withdraw my offer to buy Exclusivity Jetliners."

"What?" Roger's voice cracked over the line. "You were thrilled about the offer when we last spoke just a few days ago. What's wrong? What happened to change your mind so suddenly? Did you find a better company to meet your needs? Our arrangement is completely negotiable."

"No, please, Roger. I'm sorry, but I can't really elaborate on the subject. I hate that I have to do this, but I must. I'm sorry for the trouble I'm causing you, but I have to go."

Gavin hung up the phone before Roger could grill him for more information. He did what he had to do for Jared's sake, but he didn't have to like it. Dropping his phone onto the coffee table, he got up, brushing off the questions and sympathetic looks of Sabine and his family, and walked out of the room. He needed some space to mourn his dreams, privately.

* * *

It was 10:00 a.m. and Gavin had returned from the bank with the million-dollar ransom a few minutes ago. The whole family was gathered around the phone waiting for Paul's call and the instructions for today's trade-off.

Sabine hadn't slept. They had all stayed at the Brooks mansion, but even an expensive mattress with luxury linens couldn't lure her to sleep. And from the looks of it, Gavin hadn't slept, either. Never in her life had she seen him look like he did right now. His eyes were lined with exhaustion and sadness. Gray smudges circled beneath them. He wasn't frowning, but he wasn't smiling, either. He had shut everything off. She recognized that in him. There was too much to deal with, too much that could go wrong, so he had chosen to numb himself to the possibilities.

She knew it was hard on him. Not only because of his concern for Jared but what it cost him to ensure his son's safety. That jet acquisition had meant everything to him. Seeing him in the cockpit of that plane had been an eye-opening experience. She had experienced what she thought was the pinnacle of passion when she made love to Gavin. But for him, there was a higher joy, a greater pleasure.

He'd been so close to merging his work and his dreams. And he'd been forced to throw it away.

Sabine placed a reassuring hand on his knee, and he covered it with his own. The warmth of his skin against hers chased away the fears that threatened from the corners of her mind. She wouldn't allow herself to indulge those thoughts. She'd be no good to her son if she was a hysterical mess.

As much as she'd yelled at Gavin, and blamed him for this whole mess, she was glad to have him here with her during this. No one should have to deal with this sort of thing alone. He had handled everything, and well. There were benefits to having a take-charge man in her life, even when it was sometimes frustrating.

Gavin would do whatever it took to see that their son came home safely. Jared was their number one priority.

The phone rang. The loud sound was amplified in the silent room, sending Sabine straight up out of her seat. Gavin calmly reached out and hit the button for the speakerphone. Sabine hated listening to only half the conversation and had asked him to let her listen this time, as well.

"Yes?"

"I'm surprised, Gavin." Paul's voice boomed through the speaker. "You've done everything I've asked so far without a whisper to the police. My father was quite disappointed that your deal fell through. It was hard not to laugh in his face. You've been so cooperative you must really care about this brat. Funny, considering you've only known about him for two weeks."

Sabine fought back her urge to scream profanities into the phone. They were too close to getting Jared home safely. She could say or do whatever she wanted after that.

"I've got the money," Gavin said, ignoring his taunts. "What now?"

"Meet me in an hour in Washington Square Park. I'll be waiting by the arch with junior. You hand over the backpack, I hand over the kid."

"I'll be there."

"If I so much as smell a cop, we're done. And so is the kid."

Paul hung up, leaving them all in a stunned silence. After a moment, Celia started crying. Byron put his arm around her.

"Don't worry, dear. He doesn't have the nerve to actually hurt Jared, no matter what he says."

Gavin stood up and nodded. "He's right. Roger told me once that Paul didn't have enough ambition to get out of bed before noon most days. This is just the quickest, easiest way to make some money and get his father to do what he wants." He slung the backpack with the money onto his shoulder. "I'd better go."

Sabine leaped up, as well. "I'm going with you."

Gavin's jaw tightened. He looked as though he wanted to argue with her, but he didn't. Gavin might be able to get his way when it came to unimportant things, but that was because most times, Sabine didn't care. She cared about this, and she wouldn't take no for an answer.

"Okay. Let's go."

Sabine grabbed her own red backpack. It had a change of clothes, Pull-Ups, dry cereal, Jared's favorite stuffed dinosaur and one of his trucks. She wanted to have everything she needed to clean him up and comfort him the minute she could finally get herself to let go.

Gavin had a car drive them downtown. It let them off about a block from the park and would circle until he called to be picked up. If all went well, this shouldn't take long.

Sabine's heart was pounding wildly in her chest as they walked through the park and headed toward the arch. She could barely hear the sounds of the traffic and people surrounding them. Gavin clutched her hand in his, steadying and guiding her to the rendezvous point.

They were about five minutes early. She didn't know what Paul Simpson looked like, but Jared was nowhere in sight.

The minutes ticked by. Anxiously waiting. Then she heard it.

"Mommy!"

Like an arrow through her brain, Sabine immediately recognized the voice of her child amid the chaos of downtown. Her head turned sharply to the left. There, an older man was walking toward them carrying Jared in his arms.

She broke into a sprint, closing the gap between them. It wasn't part of the plan, but Sabine didn't care. She could hear Gavin running behind her. She stopped herself short of the man, who looked nothing like she expected him to. He was in his late fifties easily, in a nice suit. He also immediately lifted Jared from his hip and handed him into her arms.

Something about this didn't seem right, but it didn't matter. All that mattered was the warm, snuggling body of her baby back in her arms. Jared clung to her neck, his breathing a little labored as she nearly squeezed the life out of him. When she could finally ease up, she inspected her son for signs of his abduction. He was clean. Rosy-cheeked. Smiling. He actually didn't appear to think anything was awry.

What the hell was really going on?

"Roger?"

Sabine pried her attention away to listen to Gavin's conversation. Roger? That was Paul's father. Was he involved in this, too?

"Gavin, I am so sorry. You have no idea how disturbed I was to find out what was really going on. My son…" His voice trailed off. "It's inexcusable. There are no words to express how horrified I am. This must have been a day of pure hell for you both."

"What happened, Roger? We were supposed to be meeting Paul here." Gavin's dark eyes flickered over Sabine and Jared, but he didn't dare try to hold his son. He'd have to pry him from Sabine's dead arms.

"After your call last night, I got concerned. When I went into the office this morning, I heard Paul talking to someone in the day care center of our offices. He doesn't have children, so there was no reason for him to be there. Later, I overheard him talking on the phone to you. After he hung up, I confronted him and he confessed everything to me. My wife and I have been concerned about him for a while, but you never believe your children could ever do something as horrible as this."

"Where is he now?"

"He's in one of my jets on his way to a very expensive long-term rehab facility in Vermont. It was that or I disinherited him. If you want to press charges, I completely understand. I can give you the facility address for the police to pick him up. I just wanted to start getting him help right away. It seems he had more problems than even I knew, including an expensive drug habit. He owed his dealer quite a bit and had worked out a deal where he would let them use our planes to import and export drugs. That was the only reason he wanted the company. Can you imagine?"

"I'm sorry to hear that, Roger."

The old man shook his head sadly and looked over at Jared. It must be hard to know your child did something terrible when all you can see is them when they were little.

"I want you to know your little boy was in the best possible care the entire time he was gone. Paul put him in the Exclusivity Jetliners day care center. We run a twenty-four-hour facility for our employees who might have to go on long flights or overnight trips. Jared spent the last day playing with the other children. I personally guarantee there's not a scratch on him."

Sabine felt a wave of relief wash over her. No wonder Jared seemed perfectly contented. He thought he had spent the day at school with new friends and had no clue he was a kidnapping victim. Thank goodness for that. She ran her palm over his head, messing up the soft, dark hairs and standing them on end.

Jared rubbed his hair back down with both hands. "Dinosaur?" he asked.

Sabine crouched down, settling him on his feet and pulling her bag off her shoulder. "He's right here." She pulled out the plush triceratops from their trip to the American Museum of Natural History.

Jared happily hugged the dinosaur and leaned against her leg. He wasn't traumatized by the whole ordeal, but Mommy was gone a little too long for his taste. She wasn't going to be out of his sight for a while, and she knew exactly how he felt.

"I want to make this up to you," Roger said. He was shuffling awkwardly in his loafers. "At least I want to try. I doubt anything can make it better."

"Don't beat yourself up over this, Roger. You can't control what your kids do when they're adults."

"No, Gavin. I'm taking responsibility for this whole mess. I kept waiting for him to grow up, and I let things go too far. Now I want to change what I can. If you're still interested, I want to make sure you get these planes you're after. There's no way in hell I want my son to ever have his hands in the company—rehab or no. Because of everything that happened, I'd like to sell it to you for twenty percent less than we previously negotiated. How's that sound?"

Sabine watched Gavin's eyes widen in surprise. Twenty percent of the money they were talking about was apparently a huge amount. She couldn't even imagine it.

"Roger, I—"

"And I'll throw in *Beth*."

"No." Gavin shook his head. "Absolutely not. That's your private jet. You named it after your wife!"

Roger smiled and patted Gavin on the shoulder. "My first wife," he clarified. "She's not a part of the Exclusivity Jetliners fleet, I know. But I want to give her to you. Not to BXS, but to *you*. Even if the merger is off the table. I know you've always wanted your own jet, and it doesn't get much better than my *Beth,* I assure you."

"What about you?" Gavin asked.

"I'll take some of the money I make off the sale and maybe I'll buy a smaller plane. I don't need such a big one anymore. Anyway, I don't want to give Paul too many options. Maybe I'll just get a nice yacht instead and take the missus to Monaco."

"Are you sure?"

"Absolutely. I'll have my lawyers redraft the agreement and we'll be back on for Tuesday." Roger smiled and looked down at Jared with a touch of sadness in his eyes. "Again, I'm sorry about all of this. Please, take your son home and enjoy your afternoon with him."

Then he leaned in closer to Gavin. "And for the love of God, stop by the bank and get that cash put back someplace safe. You can't just walk around with a million dollars in a backpack."

Twelve

"Well," Gavin said, breaking the long silence. "Tomorrow I'm going to call the Realtor and let her know that the apartment overlooking Washington Square Park is out."

"Out? Why?" Sabine asked from the seat beside him. The town car had picked them up after Roger left and was taking them back uptown to his apartment.

"I'm not paying five million dollars for a place that will do nothing but remind you of all of this every time you look out the window. This location is tainted."

Sabine sighed. "We looked at over half a dozen apartments last week, and that was the only one I really liked. I understand your concerns, but I hate to start over."

Thankfully, Gavin had no intention of putting her through all that again. There was only one apartment she needed to tour. It had taken him a long time to come to this conclusion, but now his mind was made up. "We're not. A place has come available that no one knows about yet. I think you're really going to love it."

Her brows arched in question, but she didn't press him. At least not now. She was too busy holding a squirming Jared in her lap. After the past twenty-four hours of hell, she probably didn't think apartment hunting was high on their agenda. She would question him later.

Besides, they hadn't spoken—really spoken—since their fight on the beach. They were angry with one another and then they set that aside while they focused on getting Jared back. Now, with all of that behind them, they had nothing to do but deal with each other and the fallout of their heated and regretful words.

Gavin wasn't ready to start that awkward conversation yet. He was much happier to watch Sabine and Jared interact as they drove home. Occasionally she leaned down and inhaled the scent of his baby shampoo and smiled, very nearly on the verge of tears. How could she ever have thought he could split the two of them up? It was an impossible task.

And as time went by, splitting Gavin from Sabine and Jared was an even more impossible task.

He'd signed off on the custody agreements because they were fair and reasonable, but he didn't like them. He wouldn't see Jared nearly enough. And aside from the occasional custody trade-off, nowhere in the pile of paperwork did it say how often he would get to see Sabine. There was no such thing as visitation with the mother.

At this point, she might not want anything else to do with him. They had both said terrible things to each other. He hadn't meant a word of it. He'd been hurt by her blame and flung the most convenient insults he could find. He could tell her that. But he knew Sabine. She wouldn't pay any attention to his apologies. They were just words, and she had told him more than once that actions spoke louder.

Now was the time for action.

The car finally pulled up outside of the Ritz-Carlton. He ushered them both inside through the crowd of tourists and over to the residential elevator. He swiped the card that had special access to his floor of the hotel. In his apartment with the door locked, Gavin finally felt secure again. His family was safe and intact and he was never going to let them out of his sight again.

Once they settled in, he called his parents to let them know Jared was okay. He should've called from the car, but he needed time to mentally unwind and process everything that happened.

Jared was playing with his dinosaur on the floor when he got off the phone. Sabine was staring out the window at Central Park, her arms crossed protectively over her chest.

"Sabine?" She turned to look at him, an expression of sadness on her face. "Are you okay?"

She nodded softly. "Yes. I wanted to tell you that I'm sorry about everything I said to you. I was upset and scared when I found out something had happened to Jared. Blaming you was the easiest thing to do. It was wrong of me. Your son was in danger, too."

"I said things I didn't mean, too."

"Yes, but you were right. I was being selfish. I was so afraid of not having Jared all to myself that I kept him from you. I shouldn't have done that. I'm glad that Clay saw me and told you about him. It was a step I couldn't make on my own. I'm really glad you're going to be a part of his life."

"What about your life?"

Sabine's eyes narrowed. "Of course Jared is already a huge part of my life. Any more, he is my life."

Gavin took a few steps closer to her. "I wasn't talking about Jared. I was talking about me. Will I get to be a part of your life, too?"

She sighed and let her gaze drop to the floor. "I don't know, Gavin. The last few weeks have been nice, but it has been a lot, and fast. We have a lifetime of sharing our son. I don't want anything to mess that up. I know how important he is to you."

"*You're* important to me," he emphasized. "Both of you. Not just Jared. All this time, all that we've shared together these weeks… It wasn't just about our son or wooing you into giving me what I wanted. You know that, right?"

Sabine looked up at him, her pale green eyes still sad and now, a touch wearier than before. "I want to believe that, Gavin. Truly, I do. But how can I know anything about our relationship when you won't tell me how you feel? You'd rather let me walk away than tell me you want me to stay. I can't spend all our time together guessing. I need you to talk to me."

"You know that's hard for me. I've never been good at voicing my feelings. I've spent my whole life watching people walk away and never come back. My parents were always busy, foisting me and my siblings off on one nanny after the next until I was old enough for boarding school. They were so worried about keeping up appearances that I changed schools every few years to move on to a more prestigious program. It didn't take long for me to learn to keep my distance from everyone."

"Not everyone is going to leave you, Gavin."

"You did. You said that you would've stayed if I had asked, but how do I know that for certain? What if I told them how I felt and they left anyway? I'm not good with words. Can't I just show you how I feel?"

"More kisses? More gifts and fancy dinners? That doesn't mean anything to me. I need more, Gavin. I need to hear the words coming from your lips."

He reached out for her hand. "I'm offering more. But first, please, I want to show you something." He tugged gently until she followed him down the hallway toward Jared's newly renovated bedroom.

"You already showed me Jared's room."

"I know. This time I want to show you the other room."

Gavin turned the knob and pushed open the door to what used to be his office. When he flipped on the light switch, he heard Sabine gasp beside him.

"Remember in the car when I said that I knew of an available property that you would love? This is it. I had the old office done up for you. An art studio just for you to work. You don't have to share it with a toddler or storage boxes or cleaning supplies. It's all yours for you to do whatever you like."

Sabine stepped ahead of him into the large, open room. He'd had the hardwood floors refinished. The walls were painted a soft, matte green very close to the color of her eyes. "The consultant I worked with told me that this shade of green was a good choice for an art studio because it wouldn't influence the color of your work and would provide enough light with the off-white ceilings."

There was one large window that let in plenty of natural light and several nonfluorescent fixtures that he was told were good for art. A leather love seat sat along one wall. Several cabinets lined the other, each filled with every painting supply he could order. Several easels were already set up with blank canvases perched on them, and a few framed paintings were hanging on the walls.

"That shade of green also looked wonderful with the paintings I had of yours."

"It's beautiful. Perfect." Sabine approached one of the three canvases hanging on the wall and let her finger run along the large wooden frame. "I didn't know you had bought any of my work. Why didn't you tell me?"

"Because I bought the pieces after you left me. It was my way of keeping you in my life, I guess."

She spun on her heel to face him, her brow knit together with excitement tampered by confusion. "When did you decide to do all this?"

"Three years ago."

"What?" she gasped.

"The room was nearly finished when you broke it off. I was planning on asking you to move in with me and giving you the room as a housewarming gift. I decided to go ahead and complete it, and then I didn't have the heart to do anything else with it. I've just kept the door shut."

"You wanted me to move in with you?" Sabine's hands dropped helplessly at her sides. "I wish to God you would've said something. I didn't think I mattered to you. I loved you, but I thought I was a fool."

"I was the fool for letting you walk away. I wanted you here with me then, and I was too afraid to admit to myself that I still wanted you here with me now. I would've bought you any apartment you chose, but I knew you were meant to be here with me."

"Why didn't you tell me about it when you showed me Jared's new room?"

Gavin took a deep breath. "I thought it was too soon to show it to you. We were slowly rebuilding our relationship. I didn't know where we would end up. I thought that I might scare you away if you saw it. Too much, too soon."

"Why would you think that?"

"You'd already laughed off my proposal and shot down any suggestion of moving in with me."

"To be fair, it wasn't much of a proposal."

"True. Which is why I worried you would think the studio was my way of trying to bribe you into moving in with me after you told me no already. It's not a bribe. It's a homecoming gift. I started working on this place years ago because I wanted it to be a home for us. Now, a home for *all* of us. Not a part-time, alternate weekends and holidays home. For every day. All three of us together."

He watched tears start welling in her eyes and didn't know if it was a good or bad sign. He decided to go with it. The moment felt right even though he wasn't as prepared as he would like to be.

"Sabine, I know I'm no good at talking about my feelings. I built this space for you because I…I love you. I loved you then and I love you now. This was the only way I could think of to show you how I felt."

"You love me?" Sabine asked with a sly smile curling her lips.

"I do. Very much."

"Then say it again," she challenged.

"I love you," he repeated, this time without hesitation. A grin of his own spread wide across his face. It was getting easier every time he said it. "Now it's your turn."

Sabine leaned into him, her green gaze focused intently on him. "I love you, Gavin," she said without a moment's indecision. Then she placed her hands on his face and leaned in to kiss him.

Gavin wrapped his arms around her, thankful to have this again after two days without her touch or her kisses to help him get through it. He'd worried that he'd ruined it again.

"I'm glad you do," he said. Gavin pulled her hands from his face and held them in his. "That will make this next part less embarrassing. I want to ask again if you'll marry me, but this time, even if the answer is no, please don't laugh. A man's ego can't take that twice."

"Okay," Sabine said, her face now perfectly solemn in preparation for his query.

Gavin dropped down to one knee, her hands still grasped in his own. "Sabine Hayes, I love you. And I love our son. I want us to be a family. There is nothing on this earth—not a jet, not money—that I want more than for you to be my wife. Will you marry me?"

Sabine could barely withstand the rush of emotions surging through her. She really was on an emotional roller coaster. She'd experienced the highest of highs and the lowest of lows all in a few hours' time. If Gavin wasn't looking up at her with dark, love-filled eyes, she might start nervously twittering with laughter again simply from the stress of it all.

But she couldn't laugh. Not this time. Gavin wanted to marry her and there was nothing funny about that.

"Yes. I will marry you."

Gavin stood back up and swept her into his arms. His mouth eagerly captured hers, sealing their agreement with a kiss that made her blood sizzle through her veins. She wanted to make love to him on the leather couch of her new studio. The sooner she could start creating memories in her new home, the better.

Of course, that would have to wait for nap time.

Instead, she looked up into the dark eyes of her fiancé. The man she loved. The father of her child. There, in his arms, everything felt right. This is what she'd missed, the thing that made all those other apartments seem cold and unappealing.

"Gavin, do you know why I didn't like any of the apartments we looked at?"

He gave her a lopsided smile in response to her unexpected question. "You wanted crown molding and granite countertops?"

"No. Guess again."

He shrugged. "I'm out of guesses. Why didn't you like them?"

"Because they were all missing something—*you*."

Gavin laughed. "Of course. There's only one apartment in Manhattan that comes equipped with Gavin Brooks. It's a very exclusive address. The only way to get into the place is through marriage."

"Well, wouldn't you know that THE Gavin Brooks just asked me to be his wife?"

He picked up her left hand and eyed the bare ring finger. "This won't do. The first thing everyone will do when you tell them we're engaged is look at your hand. We need to get you an engagement ring."

"Right now?"

"We're two blocks away from Tiffany's. Why not right now?"

Sabine sighed. It had been an exciting couple of

days. Too exciting if you asked her. She was happy to spread out some of the big moments to later in the week. "There's no rush. I know you're good for it. There's a million dollars in cash lying around on the living room floor in a JanSport."

"Okay, you win. What about tomorrow?"

"I have to work tomorrow morning."

Gavin eyed her with dismay. "No, you don't."

"Yes, I do. I'm not going to abandon my wonderful, pregnant boss when she needs me. You're the one that suggested a vacation. I at least have to stay at the store long enough for her to take one."

"What about if we go early, before the boutique opens?"

"Okay," Sabine relented. If he wanted so badly to put a dangerously expensive rock on her hand, she would let him. "But make sure you don—"

"Spider-Man!"

Sabine and Gavin turned to find Jared standing in the doorway of his new bedroom. He flung the door the rest of the way open and charged in the space that was custom-made for a little boy with dreams of being a superhero.

The workers had done an excellent job on the room. It was just as Gavin had described. Red walls, a loft with a rope swing for an adventurous young boy, and a comic-book motif sure to please. All it needed was his favorite toys from their place in Brooklyn and it would be perfect.

Jared crawled up on the new bed, bouncing ever so slightly on the new Spider-Man comforter. "Big bed!"

"Yep, it's a big boy bed."

"Mine?"

"It is," Gavin replied. "Do you like it?"

Jared flipped two thumbs up. "Love Spider-Man!"

Sabine was nearly overwhelmed by the joy and excitement on their small son's face. Gavin turned to look at her and frowned when he noted the tears pooling in her eyes.

"And I love you," she said.

"More than Spider-Man?" Gavin asked.

"Oh, yeah," she replied, leaning in to kiss him and prove her point.

Epilogue

Sabine was exhausted. There wasn't really another word to describe the state a woman was in immediately following childbirth. The messy business was over. The doctors and nurses had cleared out and the family went home. Now it was just Sabine and Gavin in a quiet hospital suite.

Well, make that just Sabine, Gavin *and* the brand-new Miss Elizabeth Anne Brooks in a quiet hospital suite.

Beth made her arrival at 4:53 p.m., weighing seven pounds, two ounces and shrieking with the finest set of lungs to ever debut at St. Luke's Hospital. They named her after Gavin's private plane—*Beth*—and Sabine's mother, with whom she'd recently reconciled.

Gavin's parents, siblings and the housekeeper had left a few hours ago with Jared in tow. Their son had been very excited to see his new sister, but the novelty wore off pretty quickly when she didn't do anything but sleep.

He insisted that Grandpa and Grandma take him for ice cream and when visiting hours ended, they relented.

It had been a long day filled with excitement, nerves, joy and pain. And now, she was enjoying a private moment she would remember for her whole life.

Gavin was beside her in the reclining chair. Beth was bundled up in a white blanket with pastel stripes. She was perfect, tiny and pink with Sabine's nose. The nurses had put a hat on to keep her head warm. It hid away the wild mohawk of dark hair she'd been born with. Gavin said her crazy hair was from Sabine, too. Beth had fallen asleep with her small hand clutching his pinky finger, content, warm and safe in her daddy's arms.

But the best part was watching Gavin.

The past nine months had been an adventure for her husband. Since he'd missed out on her first pregnancy, Gavin wanted to be a part of every moment from sonograms to Lamaze classes. Sometimes she wondered if he regretted getting so immersed in the details of the process.

He could handle running shipping empires and flying jets, but preparing for the arrival of a new baby—and a girl at that—nearly did him in. During labor, he was wide-eyed and panicked. Occasionally even a little green around the gills. It was pretty adorable.

Then she was born, shouting her displeasure to everyone in the maternity ward. Of course, Sabine looked at her baby first, cataloging fingers and toes and noting how beautiful and perfect she was. But the moment Beth was laid on her chest, Sabine's eyes went to Gavin. The expression on his face was priceless. It was quite literally love at first sight.

And now, while he held her, a marching band could parade through the room and Gavin probably wouldn't notice. He couldn't tear his gaze away from his daughter. It was as though the answers to all the questions in the universe were wrapped up in that blanket. It was the most precious thing Sabine had ever seen.

"You're my hero."

Sabine didn't realize Gavin was looking at her until he spoke. "Your hero?"

"Absolutely. You were amazing today." Gavin stood slowly so he didn't wake their daughter and carried Beth over to her.

Sabine accepted the bundle and smiled up at him. "Eh, piece of cake. I think I only threatened your life once."

"Twice, but who's counting?" Gavin eased down to sit on the edge of the bed and put his arm around her shoulders. "Seriously, though, I don't know how you did it. *Before.* With Jared. I mean, I knew that *I* had missed a lot, but one thing I never really considered was how it was for you. To do this all alone…"

It certainly was different this time. Before, one of her gallery friends came by the next day. That was it. This time, she had an entire cheering squad waiting in the next room, a crew in Nebraska staying up to date on Facebook and a husband holding her hand. What a difference a few years could make.

"That was the choice I made." She shrugged. "The wrong one, obviously. It was definitely better with you here."

Gavin leaned in to place a kiss on her lips and another on Beth's forehead. "I have to say I agree."

They both spent a moment looking down at their daughter. "She looks like you," Gavin said.

"That's fair since Jared looks like you. Besides, it would be unfortunate for a girl to have your chin."

"I can tell she's going to give me trouble. If she's half as beautiful and smart and talented as her mother, the boys will be lined up the block."

"She's four hours old. I don't think you need to start polishing the shotgun just yet. You've got years of ballet recitals and princess parties before we need to start worrying about that."

Gavin smiled and leaned his head against hers. "I'm looking forward to every pink, glittery second."

* * * * *

*If you liked Sabine's story,
don't miss these other novels from
Andrea Laurence*

*WHAT LIES BENEATH
MORE THAN HE EXPECTED
UNDENIABLE DEMANDS
A BEAUTY UNCOVERED
BACK IN HER HUSBAND'S BED*

All available now, from Harlequin Desire!

If you liked this
BILLIONAIRES & BABIES *novel,
watch for the next book in this
#1 bestselling Desire series,*
THE SARANTOS BABY BARGAIN
by USA TODAY *bestselling author Olivia Gates,
available May 2014.*

#2299 YOUR RANCH...OR MINE?
The Good, the Bad and the Texan • by Kathie DeNosky
Five-card draw suddenly becomes a game of hearts when professional poker player Lane Donaldson wins half a Texas ranch and discovers he's soon to be housemates with the spirited beauty who inherited the other half!

#2300 FROM SINGLE MOM TO SECRET HEIRESS
Dynasties: The Lassiters • by Kristi Gold
High-rolling lawyer Logan Whittaker tracks down a secret heiress, only to find a feisty single mom who isn't necessarily ready to join the scandal-plagued Lassiter family. But what if Hannah's real home is with him?

#2301 THE SARANTOS BABY BARGAIN
Billionaires and Babies • by Olivia Gates
Now guardian to an orphaned little girl, Andreas Sarantos wants only the best for her, which means marrying the baby's adoptive mother—his ex-wife. But their arrangement becomes less than convenient when his passion for Naomi reignites....

#2302 CAROSELLI'S ACCIDENTAL HEIR
The Caroselli Inheritance • by Michelle Celmer
Forced to marry and produce an heir, Antonio Caroselli is about to say "I do" when his ex shows up—pregnant! He's always wanted Lucy, but will she believe in their love after she finds out about the terms of the will?

#2303 THE LAST COWBOY STANDING
Colorado Cattle Barons • by Barbara Dunlop
After a disastrous first meeting, Colorado rancher Travis and city-gal Danielle don't expect to cross paths again. But when they end up in a Vegas hotel suite together, there's no denying the depths of their desires.

#2304 A MERGER BY MARRIAGE
Las Vegas Nights • by Cat Schield
When spunky hotel executive Violet Fontaine inherits a rival company's stock, she helps the enigmatic JT Stone reclaim control of his family's company the only way she can—by marrying him!

REQUEST YOUR FREE BOOKS!
2 FREE NOVELS PLUS 2 FREE GIFTS!

HARLEQUIN®

Desire

ALWAYS POWERFUL, PASSIONATE AND PROVOCATIVE

YES! Please send me 2 FREE Harlequin Desire® novels and my 2 FREE gifts (gifts are worth about $10). After receiving them, if I don't wish to receive any more books, I can return the shipping statement marked "cancel." If I don't cancel, I will receive 6 brand-new novels every month and be billed just $4.55 per book in the U.S. or $4.99 per book in Canada. That's a savings of at least 13% off the cover price! It's quite a bargain! Shipping and handling is just 50¢ per book in the U.S. and 75¢ per book in Canada.* I understand that accepting the 2 free books and gifts places me under no obligation to buy anything. I can always return a shipment and cancel at any time. Even if I never buy another book, the two free books and gifts are mine to keep forever.

225/326 HDN F4ZN

Name _____ (PLEASE PRINT)

Address _____ Apt. #

City _____ State/Prov. _____ Zip/Postal Code _____

Signature (if under 18, a parent or guardian must sign)

Mail to the **Harlequin® Reader Service:**
IN U.S.A.: P.O. Box 1867, Buffalo, NY 14240-1867
IN CANADA: P.O. Box 609, Fort Erie, Ontario L2A 5X3

Want to try two free books from another line?
Call 1-800-873-8635 or visit www.ReaderService.com.

* Terms and prices subject to change without notice. Prices do not include applicable taxes. Sales tax applicable in N.Y. Canadian residents will be charged applicable taxes. Offer not valid in Quebec. This offer is limited to one order per household. Not valid for current subscribers to Harlequin Desire books. All orders subject to credit approval. Credit or debit balances in a customer's account(s) may be offset by any other outstanding balance owed by or to the customer. Please allow 4 to 6 weeks for delivery. Offer available while quantities last.

Your Privacy—The Harlequin® Reader Service is committed to protecting your privacy. Our Privacy Policy is available online at www.ReaderService.com or upon request from the Harlequin Reader Service.

We make a portion of our mailing list available to reputable third parties that offer products we believe may interest you. If you prefer that we not exchange your name with third parties, or if you wish to clarify or modify your communication preferences, please visit us at www.ReaderService.com/consumerschoice or write to us at Harlequin Reader Service Preference Service, P.O. Box 9062, Buffalo, NY 14269. Include your complete name and address.

HDDIR13R

*The Lassiter family lawyer has some surprise news for one
stunning woman...*

She looked prettier than a painted picture come to life.
Yep. Trouble with a capital *T* if he didn't get his mind back
on business.

"After you learn the details of your share of the Lassiter
fortune, you'll be able to buy me dinner next time." *Next
time?* Man, he was getting way ahead of himself, and that
was totally out of character for his normally cautious self.

Hannah looked about as surprised as he felt over the
comment. "That all depends on if I actually agree to accept
my share, and that's doubtful."

He couldn't fathom anyone in their right mind turning
down that much money. But before he had a chance to toss
out an opinion, their waiter showed up with their entrées.

Logan ate his food with the gusto of a field hand, while
Hannah basically picked at hers, the same way she had with
the salad. By the time they were finished, and the plates were
cleared, he had half a mind to invite her into the nearby bar
to discuss business. But dark and cozy wouldn't help rein in
his libido.

HDEXP0414

Hannah tossed her napkin aside and folded her hands before her. "Okay, we've put this off long enough. Tell me the details."

Logan took a drink of water in an attempt to rid the dryness in his throat. "The funds are currently in an annuity. You have the option to leave it as is and take payments. Or you can claim the lump sum. Your choice."

"How much?" she said after a few moments.

He noticed she looked a little flushed and decided retiring to the bar might not be a bad idea after all. "Maybe we should go into the lounge so you can have a drink before I continue."

Frustration showed in her expression. "I don't need a drink."

He'd begun to think he might. "Just a glass of wine to take the edge off."

She leaned forward and nailed him with a glare. *"How much?"*

"Five million dollars."

"I believe I will have that drink now."

Don't miss
FROM SINGLE MOM TO SECRET HEIRESS
Available May 2014
Wherever Harlequin® Desire books are sold.

HARLEQUIN®

Desire

ALWAYS POWERFUL, PASSIONATE AND PROVOCATIVE.

THE SARANTOS BABY BARGAIN
Billionaires and Babies
by Olivia Gates

Now guardian to his orphaned niece, Andreas Sarantos
wants only the best for her, which means marrying the
baby's adoptive mother—his ex-wife. But their arrangement
becomes less than convenient when his passion for
Naomi reignites....

Look for THE SARANTOS BABY BARGAIN
in May 2014, from Harlequin Desire!
Wherever books and ebooks are sold.

Don't miss other scandalous titles from the
Billionaires and Babies miniseries,
available now wherever books and ebooks are sold.

HIS LOVER'S LITTLE SECRET
by Andrea Laurence

DOUBLE THE TROUBLE
by Maureen Child

YULETIDE BABY SURPRISE
by Catherine Mann

CLAIMING HIS OWN
by Elizabeth Gates

A BILLIONAIRE FOR CHRISTMAS
by Janice Maynard

THE NANNY'S SECRET
by Elizabeth Lane

SNOWBOUND WITH A BILLIONAIRE
by Jules Bennett

HD73314